a thirst for
rain

a thirst for
rain

ROSLYN CARRINGTON

KENSINGTON BOOKS
http://www.kensingtonbooks.com

KENSINGTON BOOKS are published by

Kensington Publishing Corp.
850 Third Avenue
New York, NY 10022

Copyright © 1999 by Roslyn Carrington

Library of Congress Card Catalogue Number: 98-075688
ISBN 1-57566-446-1

First Printing: September, 1999
10 9 8 7 6 5 4 3 2 1

Printed in the United States of America

A Thirst for Rain is dedicated with love to my grandparents.
I thank Frederick Hull, for teaching me to love words: the sound of them, the feel of them, and the taste of them, and for raising me to always ask, "Why?"
I thank Rosa Hull, for teaching me to hold on to my sense of self, even in the face of doubt.
I thank Vas Carrington, for passing on her quick laughter, and for protecting me with her prayers during the times when my curiosity led me to court danger.
Finally, I thank the late Harold Theodore Carrington—although we scarcely had enough time to get to know each other, his legacy to me was a thirst for knowledge, which is perhaps the most important gift one can give a child.

april

Jacob

The walls of Jacob's small room were papered in a most unusual fashion: with the yellowed leaves of a large Bible. Row after row, carefully, like a craftsman laying tiles, the previous tenant had laid the pages side by side, from the floor to the ceiling, turning them lengthwise along the skirting and the window-frames for contrast. Whether the intention had been to ward off some curse, incur blessings, or simply to satisfy an unusual sense of style, Jacob could not tell. He did, however, welcome the digression from the ordinary that they presented, the promise of something to do, something with which he could fill the endless idle days between customers.

The pages had been laid in random order, with no regard for the precedence which had been divinely inspired for each book of Scripture. It was as though the layer of the paper tiles had somehow escaped the rhythmic Sunday school chanting that is inflicted upon every small child, and thus did not know the sequence of the books, no Matthew-Mark-Luke-John, no order, no place-for-everything-and-everything-in-its-place. Instead, the horrors of the Apocalypse lay next to Boaz's wooing of Ruth, on the wall above the narrow steel bed. At the door, running down the left side, Samson was setting the foxes' tails alight; above that, Rachel wept.

Jacob's wallpaper entranced him. He spent hours on his knees in a parodic attitude of prayer, ignoring the clamouring spasmodic pain in his ruined left leg, peering down into a corner, shifting bed, table, chair, to reach an elusive page. He made no attempt to rationalise, to seek out the page which may have followed the one that he had just read; instead, he took the pages as they had been given to him. On one day he would read at random, moving from wall to wall. On another he moved carefully from one page to its neighbour, then on to the next, enjoying in particular the pages upon which his own name appeared.

Once in a while he wondered what could possibly be printed on the backs of the pages, which had been stuck firmly to the wall with fishy brown glue, but this was idle curiosity, a passing thought. He accepted the serendipity which had decided that this side would lie face up while condemning the other to remain forever hidden from view as the result of simple caprice, and let it be.

Jacob, though just forty-eight, felt long past his prime. He was a huge, burly man, with black dense skin and thick ursine limbs. The quickness of his black, intelligent eyes was in startling contrast to his slow, often painful gait. He had lived his youth in glorious notoriety in the sleepy old town of Sangre Grande in the eastern countryside of Trinidad. He had been the neighborhood bad-john, a romantic Zorro-like hero of the barrack-yards who drank and swaggered and cursed with the best of them.

His stickfighting prowess had been a drawing card for the illegal bloodsport, and for years people gathered in furtive groups deep in the forest to watch Jacob mercilessly bring an opponent to his knees under the brunt of his huge, polished staff.

Jacob loved the stickfighting, not out of any innate aggression or hatred of humanity. Far from it. He loved the dark seclusion of the woods, the secrecy of the activity, the fear of being caught and hauled before the magistrate, the roar of the excited crowds and the frenzied shouts of *"Bois!"* as he bludgeoned his opponent into unconsciousness. He loved the adulation, the respectful whispers of *"Maître"* as he passed. He was indeed a master of the stickfight, and his wooden staff, the *bois* that he had fashioned by his own hand out of sturdy mahogany, hung on two hooks over his bed at night. Children broke into mock battles as he passed, re-enacting some of his more celebrated battles, telling each other time and again how he brought such and such a person to his knees by hitting him just *so*.

But the *gayelle,* the stickfighting ring, was not the only arena for Jacob's conquests. The women, entranced by the circumference of his matted chest, by his bad-john reputation, his boisterous good humour, and his rumored indefatigable lust, rivaled each other for his attentions. They laid their charms before him like bazaar vendors displaying their wares, bribing him with hot baked goods, clear bottles of bush-rum from their backyard stills, and gifts of shirts and trousers which, as they lost no opportunity to tell him, they had made with their own two hands.

Jacob accepted their attentions as an inevitable and pleasurable burden, and meandered aimlessly through his youth as through an orchard, plucking the ripest of fruit, and devouring just as avidly those that fell at his feet.

When the law cracked down on the stickfighting, imposing harsher penalties for an activity that Jacob considered little more than a harmless noble sport, Jacob eventually sought legitimate employment. With his size and reputation he had easily found himself a job as foreman of a gravel quarry in the east, and there he exercised his authority with a heavy hand but an unquestionable sense of fair play.

The day a misplaced stick of dynamite went off without warning, Jacob was standing right beside it. What followed were two excruciating and laborious years of surgery and rehabilitation. Gone were the glory days of the *gayelle.* Gone, too, were the days of earning his living as a man, with dignity, and by the sweat of his brow. He was reduced to living like an old man on disability pension, without pride, without power.

In his shame he skulked out of Sangre Grande one night

when the moon was full and the *gayelle* was spattered with the blood of the fool who had challenged the strapping young buck who had replaced him, the new *Maître*. With the lure of the moonlit arena greater to the gamblers and sport-lovers than the fear of a good beating by the police, the forest thronged, vibrating with the excited cries of *"Bois!"*

He took what little was left of his manhood and migrated to Port of Spain, where he had been these six years, moving from rooming house to rooming house, supplementing his disability pay by doing passable leather-work, repairing shoes and handbags on his front porch.

So here he was now, four months in his new home, and still aloof, not entirely a part of the communal yard in which he lived. The yard, a cramped enclosure which was home to three other families, stood in the deep valley of St. Ann's, north of the city's wide, rolling Queen's Park Savannah. It was a quiet neighborhood, clean and well kept, standing a respectful distance away from some of the better St. Ann's neighborhoods like Sydenham and Coblentz.

April wasn't promising to be so bad, though the dryness had claimed the Savannah, leaving the low-cut grass that covered the sprawling park a dismal brown, and sending blankets of dust across it. But the river that ran down the crevasse that bisected St. Ann's kept the valley well watered. The bush fires were small and easily controlled, and as yet no houses had been threatened. The season looked hopeful.

The yard in which Jacob lived enclosed four living spaces within a sagging chain-link fence. A long unimaginative building held the three larger units, which stood in a row at the centre of the yard, and Jacob's unit, tiny by comparison, stood a little to one side and further back from the road. Jacob had chosen it because it was separate. It allowed him to remain apart from the lives of the others while not costing him what a house on its own would have cost. From where he sat, he could watch the stream of people that passed in the road, watch the neighbour boy throw cricket balls against the wall, and watch Myra and her daughter pass in and out of the apartment next door.

"Yes, Lord," Jacob sighed to himself as his heavy hands worked a piece of tough leather. "Yes, Father, thank you for the day." He wasn't quite sure whether he was indeed addressing any divine being, unsure even as to whether any such person actually existed. He was merely parroting the verbal meanderings of the grandmother who had raised him, a habit into which he lapsed when he was deep in concentration. "Yes, yes, yes," he said, and twisted the leather viciously.

The shuffling sound of aimless steps caught his attention for a moment. He looked up. "Evening, Mr. Cole," he said politely to the old man who was peering at him through the chain-link fence a few yards away. "You looking fine today."

"You want to cross the road?" the old man croaked, focusing with difficulty through pebble-glass spectacles. "I could cross you over, you know."

Jacob shook his head, "It's all right, Mr. Cole. I'm fine right here."

"You sure you don't want to cross the road? I could cross you if you want, you know."

Jacob shook his head abruptly but didn't reply. Eventually the old man turned slowly and shuffled back to the curb to take up his former position. The children would soon be passing on their way from school; it was his duty to help.

Sebastian

Sebastian stood at the side of the road, back hunched, staring up at the corner to his left. This was the corner that the droves of children would round on their way from school, chattering and laughing, talking loudly, shouting, shoving. And when they came, he would help them across the road.

His buckled spine poked through the clean, worn shirt that his daughter had given him to put on just this morning. The shirt was one that he liked very much, pale orange with narrow dark stripes, like a soldier's stripes, fine and neat. His shirttails were tucked into the waist of his pants, neat, like they should be. The black plastic belt that encircled his thin waist almost twice struggled manfully to keep the pants from slipping off his hipless form. An ancient gray fedora kept the sun out of his fading eyes, and a red, folded umbrella poked up out of his back pocket.

Sebastian kept a protective hand on the handle of his baby pram. It was a real pram, just large enough for a child. He didn't remember where he got it, but it was big and dark green and held all that was precious to him, and he didn't want anyone to try to steal it, no siree. He tried to keep one eye on the street corner and one on the pram. It was an uncomfortable effort.

Neatly arrayed in the pram were his newspapers, each folded carefully once, stacked one atop the other, just so.

There was his doll's head, a dirty, staring thing whose eyes never closed and who had been made half bald by some malicious child. He'd propped the head on its own little pillow.

Two empty soft drink bottles lay side by side next to the head, and on top of these, a handkerchief, blue and gray, with a lovely striped pattern. There was a handful of pretty pebbles that he had collected at the beach, or down by the river, a place that he visited whenever Myra's back was turned. He also kept a spoon, knife (Myra would scream at him if she knew he had that!), and fork, just in case he ever got hungry. Whenever he found a little treasure, a coin, a leaf, an empty juice box, he would lovingly make room for it in his green pram.

Sebastian heard the sound of childish laughter and straightened as best he could. It was well after three, and the first wave of schoolchildren was descending upon the street. He waited patiently, face cracked by a broad smile as they approached.

"You want to cross the road?" he asked the first politely. He moved to grasp her arm.

The child knew Sebastian well, and viewed him as one of the hazards of the walk to and from school. As he held her arm in his bony fingers, the other children sniggered, embarrassing her. "No," she snapped. "I don't. Leave me alone." She tore her arm out of his frail grasp and stomped by. The others laughed with a cruelty that only children know.

Sebastian smiled benignly and turned to an approaching group of boys and girls and asked them the same question.

"Crazy man! Crazy man!" they pealed with laughter and went dancing up the street. Sebastian smiled at their receding backs. He waited patiently at the side of the road under the blazing sun. More children would soon come.

A young woman alighted from an old blue taxi. Sebastian knew the taxi well: it was one of those small, rickety contraptions which plied the route between Port of Spain and St. Ann's with a load of people. Sebastian often helped the driver by standing at the corner and signaling him when it was safe to pull out into the traffic.

The driver got out and moved to open the trunk of the car, placing two large baskets onto the curb. He accepted the proffered three dollars and sped off to deliver his other passengers. The woman picked up her two baskets and smiled warmly at Sebastian.

"You want to cross the road? I can cross you over, you know." He looked at her hopefully.

The woman, who was much taller than he, bent forward and gently kissed him on the cheek. "Hello, Daddy," she said.

Sebastian looked at her in surprise, unsure of what to say. He stood, waiting.

"Dad," Myra said eventually, putting down one basket and placing her hand on her father's frail arm. "Let's go inside. The sun's so hot today."

"I'm crossing the children," he responded, looking with uncertainty beyond her to see if any others were coming.

"Let's go in now," she said soothingly, "and you can come back out when it's cooler. Later this evening, okay?" She nudged him encouragingly in the direction of the house. Smiling, Sebastian wheeled his pram around and followed her into the baked dirt yard.

Myra

Myra set her baskets down with relief, and felt around her pockets for the door key. Behind her, Sebastian hovered, knobbed fingers curled protectively around the handlebar of his pram. She cooed softly to him as she inserted the key in the lock.

"Daddy, you had a good day? Mine was okay. I didn't sell too much; month-end isn't until next week. You know people kind of short of cash this week." He wasn't much for conversation, and quite often she wasn't sure just how much he understood of what she said, but he followed the sound of her voice intently, and this reassured her. The door swung open, and she took the two heavy baskets in.

"I brought back some corn soup and some bakes for us. You hungry yet?" She set her baskets down in the small kitchen and looked around, realising that her father had not followed her in. She went back out to the porch and found him standing there, still holding on to the pram, staring up at the enormous tamarind tree that spread its branches over most of the building. With the dry season stepping up the heat, it had begun to shed its leaves, and the tiny ovals were drifting downwards like confetti, scattering themselves over the porch, the dry yard, and the gutter that ran outside the fence. Sebastian was staring upwards in wonderment at the cascade, mouth open, revealing scattered stumps of teeth.

Myra came and stood beside him, looking up. "Pretty," she agreed with his unspoken observation. "Really pretty." Then she looked at the green, brown, and gold debris on her porch and pursed her full lips. "But I'm going to have to clean it up." She bustled inside, Sebastian in tow. "First I have to put these things away."

Sebastian followed her into the kitchen. "Sit down, Daddy," she urged. He sat at the table with his thin arms folded lightly before him, watching her politely.

Myra delved into the baskets to extract several used food containers, wrappers, and serving implements. She made a good living selling food in a hut the size of a bus stop in Port of Spain, providing the simple Creole fare that appealed to the man in the street because of its generous portions, reasonable price, and the touch of a woman who knew about cooking. Her income fluctuated with that of her clients, and with payday a full five days away, sales were down a little, as her clients made do with their own bagged sandwiches.

But when things were good, and sales boomed, Myra came home late in the evening with everything sold out, smiling. On weekends she stayed late in town, selling out her steaming portions of corn soup, barley soup, hot accra and float, peppery black pudding, and homemade fruit juices and candies. On these profitable evenings, after closing up shop, she would hang around town, down on the Promenade close to the port, listening to the street musicians and throwing coins for the fire-eater. She would sit on the smooth wooden benches with a beer in her hand, enjoying the coolness of the bottle against her skin. Passersby, from boys who weren't old enough to know better to men who were but didn't, often turned their heads sharply at the sight of this beautiful woman who sat there listening to the music with her eyes closed and a beer clasped to her bosom. Those were the rare nights when she could set aside the weight of her responsibilities, when she could be alone and in control.

Tonight was not one of those nights; she was home quite early. She extracted a parcel of left-over accra and float: crisp fritters of salted fish in a sandwich of dough that had been fried in hot oil until they literally floated to the surface, swollen three times their original size. They always had her leftovers for dinner.

Men said that her linseed, seamoss, and peanut punches were 'good for the back' and enhanced their performance with women, so they often took home an extra bottle of one or the other as insurance against failure. Others, though, attributed their increased libido to the presence of Myra herself. She was a woman of uncommon good looks. Taller than most, with wide shoulders and a strong back, she had large round breasts, the firmness of which belied her thirty-five years, and a magnificent backside that balanced delicately on a fulcrum of solid, fleshy thighs. She greased her warm nutbrown skin each night with cocoa butter from the country, not the processed garbage you could get in a store, warming it first by rubbing it vigorously between her palms before applying it slowly and lovingly to her naked body.

When Slim was sober enough to find his way to her house, he would crawl gratefully into her bed, reverently inhaling the sweet odor of the balm, and devouring her glossy naked skin with his eyes. Her man would then stroke the length of a meaty leg, pinching it, as though judging cattle in a market.

Myra would laugh and stretch her legs out to him, encouraging him to feel and to explore, turning this way and that, teasing, enticing, promising. And he would tell her she was the most fucking beautiful woman in the world, and begin to tell her gravely, in explicit detail, exactly what he intended to do to her, and where, and how. She would laugh loudly with excitement and withdraw, telling him he couldn't, he shouldn't, that her daughter was in the next room, and, besides, she wasn't in the mood.

But Slim knew her well after these three years, and knew how to play her game. He would pretend to be angry, and utter threats and grab for her. She would squirm from his grasp, slippery as she was with the cocoa butter all over her, and leap around the room, dancing and laughing until she was caught and roughly tossed onto the bed, and she would scream and scream as though she were being violated, panting with excitement.

Myra held the last bottle of linseed punch in her hands, staring into space, thinking of how much Slim liked it, and how he drank it greedily, promising her that when the punch's notorious aphrodisiac effect began to swell inside him she had better watch out. She hadn't seen him in a week—more than that, probably. She thought of him, the sheer reckless worthlessness of him, the young wretch. He was probably out sniffing after some young, high-assed bitch from the city, or strung out on weed, or drunk, or out gambling.

She shook her head, wondering as she had innumerable times before how she could have let such a wastrel and pretender into her life and into her bed. *Worse,* she groaned to herself, *how did she allow him to get her pregnant?*

Instinctively, her hand moved to her thick belly. She stroked it idly, wondering how soon she would begin to show, and how, after an interval of seventeen years, she could find herself in this predicament again. She remembered the night of the conception; she was sure she could pinpoint exactly when it had happened.

It was the weekend before Carnival, and they had been out at the Savannah listening to the sweet intoxicating steel bands as they had rolled across the stage in procession, thumping out their vital, soul-possessing music. It was the final week of the monthlong series of steel-band competitions, and the thronging crowd of excited fans was dense, pressing in on them on all sides. They'd been in the thick of the undulating mass, down close to the stage in all the dust and excitement, feeling the music as it vibrated through them.

She and Slim had each had half a dozen beers, and maybe a rum or two, and by the time they returned to her yard, she was aching and wet and ready even before they hit the bed. He'd stuck his sly serpentine tongue in her ear and whispered to her nastily, and this time she'd made no effort to push him away, but had wound her legs around his back, fully clothed, returning his kisses with even hotter ones, drunk with the festival in the air and the smell of the Savannah dust on his skin and the music and his low lascivious voice. The graceful, young hard body against hers had obscured every rational thought of protection or caution; she succumbed to the unavoidable collision of their bodies.

The next day, when reason returned, she lay alone in the shambles of the bed with her arms thrown across her eyes, blotting out the light. Slim had wandered off sometime during the morning, loath as he always was to remain after his frenzy had subsided. He was not a man for idle conversation and other such post-coital niceties.

She knew then that she was pregnant. She didn't know how she knew, or why she felt it was so, but she *knew*. She had kept silent, not mentioning a word of it to Slim on any of his subsequent fleeting visits, nor to her daughter, not wanting to worry her until it was necessary. As for her father, well, it would make no difference to him one way or the other, she supposed.

"Slim better straighten up and help me mind this thing," she said of her man, shaking herself out of her reverie and busying herself washing up the empty food containers. "I'm not going through this by myself again. Not again."

As a young girl, Myra had never been one for the books, but instead had preferred to revel in the bold glances that she elicited in the young men around her. Her testing ground had been the backstreets of her native San Fernando, in the narrow, twisted streets of the hilly southland. She got her education in the darkened storefront doorways, the quiet alleys, rather than the classroom.

At Odile's age, seventeen, Myra was already pregnant with Odile, and had been forced to leave school. She'd gotten no help from the father of the child, not that she had expected any. He'd been a careless one, handsome but thoughtless and stupid and seductive and selfish. He'd lived for his prick. Thinking back for a fleeting moment, all she could remember of his face was a devilish grin that did little to mask the self-serving silliness behind it. She'd left home in the face of the wrath of a father who still had his mind back then, to the great disappointment of a mother who'd fought to instill in her daughter virtues which Myra could not fathom, let alone assimilate.

She remembered the day that she'd left, with her bulging belly barely hidden by a heavy cardigan which she drew around her in spite of the heat. Her mother had stood on the bottom step in front of their small house, watching. Sebastian had been in a roaring temper, and had even tried to prevent Myra from leaving with her own clothing. He'd paid for those clothes, he stormed, and he didn't see why they should belong on the back of some young slut who couldn't keep her legs closed. Only the tears of his wife caused him to relent and allow Myra to keep the small canvas bag of belongings that she wanted to take with her.

Myra found a job as a baker's assistant on High Street, and from time to time her father would come in, buy a quart of bread, and walk out with the brown paper bag in his fist without looking at her. Although there was another bakery just down from the street where her parents had lived, he made irregular visits to the bakery where she worked, and when he came, Myra served him silently, sometimes slipping in a small iced cupcake for her mother. It was years before they spoke again.

She raised her daughter as well as she could with what little she had, and she thought she had done admirably well. Her daughter was a child whom she knew would become something, who was already making her proud with her performance in school and on the cricket pitch. The girl was as beautiful as Myra, and held in her long limbs and solid hips the same sensuous promise that her mother had fulfilled. Myra was pleased that her efforts at rearing the child had been so successful, and that Odile was proving to be a serious, studious child, concentrating on her studies rather than on the cocky manchildren who were no doubt dangling temptation in her face. She'd gotten her into a good girls' school in Port of

Spain, where she would be laying the right kind of foundation. She was preparing to sit her Advanced Level exams in a year, and had been making all sacrifices in order to be ready. Her admission to the university depended on good results, and competition was stiff. Boys would come later, when she was old enough.

Thank God, she thought, smiling to herself, thank God Odile was different. Thank God that she had succeeded in raising her daughter so that the nature that smouldered beneath the surface had been held at bay.

Myra smiled and put her hand across her belly once again. She wondered if she were playing incubator to another beautiful, tempestuous fast-bowler, agile, strong, and swift on the cricket pitch. "We'll see," she whispered to herself, and resolved to tell Slim about the baby the next time she saw him. As for Odile, well, she would tell her when it became necessary.

Odile

Odile chose to walk home rather than hop one of the cheap battered little St. Ann's taxis that tapped their horns at her as she walked. She needed to think. It was quite late, almost five, and school had let out over two hours ago, but Myra wasn't expecting her home just yet. She'd told her mother that she was staying back in the library to do some work, and usually this was true, but not today. Odile had had more important things to do.

As she walked steadily and slowly along the bike path that ran the circumference of the Savannah, she looked down at her feet, which were demurely clad in regulation black loafers and white socks. Her heavy books, clutched close to her chest, pressed her breasts painfully flat against her rib cage.

She was tall, like her mother, with long athletic legs and a graceful gait. Her hair was carefully braided in the style that was favored by her generation—a mass of long, fine plaits that could be arranged to fall loosely about her shoulders or be gathered together and pulled back into a single bundle behind her head. The braids fell to the centre of her back, but Odile would be quick to boast to anyone that the hair was actually hers, and hadn't been bought in a store.

She walked, deep in thought, oblivious to the early-evening joggers puffing past her, and to the dogs, the lovers, the crick-eters, the traffic, the noise. She was loath to reach her destination, and even more loath to encounter her mother. Myra was a shrewd woman, in spite of her choice of lover, Odile thought. She would look right through her. The thought caused a cold, painful constriction in her chest. She was afraid, she was *sure,* that as soon as she walked into the house, Myra would take one look at her and know that she was pregnant.

Pregnant, the doctor had said. Maybe six weeks. Maybe seven. As she plodded reluctantly onward, she did some quick subtraction in her head. She had been doing the sums over and over all evening, since she left the clinic. Seven weeks.

Seven weeks. That would have made it February, around the time of the steel-band competition, or thereabouts. Carnival time. She was pretty sure that Blue was the father, quite sure, but when could it have happened? How could she have been stupid enough to let it happen? She, who had read all the books and knew what to use and how. Wryly, she reminded herself that she had never been one for caution; she was by nature a little impulsive, a taker of risks.

She remembered how this Carnival she and Blue would sneak off to the Savannah to stand at the entrance to the stands, to watch the costumed masqueraders compete on stage, and to listen to the steel bands as they let their souls waft skyward on the music that they played. She would tell her mother that she was in this study group or the other, or even steal the opportunity to escape when Myra was working late or off carousing with that ugly yellow dog of a boyfriend. And she and Blue would sway to the music and eventually run off hand-in-hand to some dark quiet place: in the Botanical Gardens, or up the low hillock overlooking the zoo, somewhere close to the Savannah where they could still hear the music of the steel bands as an accompaniment to their lovemaking.

She pursed her lips. When the truth was out, there would be hell to pay. She was grateful for once that her grandfather was no longer conversant with reality. In the days when he still possessed his faculties, he would have been enraged. He never believed that a child was too old for a whipping, and had been known to lay a hand or two on Myra even when she was fully grown and living on her own. Her grandpa would have forced her to stand and watch while he selected a fine young tamarind branch, and strip the bark from its entire length, until he held in his hands a supple, pale-green whip that cracked in the air as he tested it—*whoop!* Then he would have proceeded to flay her with it, shouting above her cries, emphasising his blows with bellows of "You . . . are . . . too . . . wicked! Wicked! Wicked!" and each blow would land like a punctuation mark. She shuddered at the image.

But Grandpa was beyond that now. His main concern, his only concern, was the traffic that passed in front of their yard. Myra, on the other hand . . . Odile sucked her teeth in disgust and frustration. Her mother still thought she was a child. She'd even bet her mother thought she was still a *virgin,* for God's sake, could you believe it? How old did she think she was, twelve?

And besides, what kind of example did Myra think she was setting anyway, carrying on like that with that half-breed boy, ten years her junior, that worthless pig that she allowed to rut her once a week, with her loud cries, as though she didn't care whether the neighbours could hear or not, as though it didn't matter that her daughter was right next door, trying to study or to sleep? Who did Myra think she was? What did she expect from her, when she set her an example like that?

Bolstered by these thoughts of righteous indignation, Odile threw back her shoulders, and trudged up the long, sloping road that led up into the heart of St. Ann's. Well, her ma would just have to accept it. And as for her classes, she would have had the baby before exams came around next year; she would just have to deal with the situation when it came. She nodded, confirming her decision to herself. She would sit her mother down and tell her. When she was good and ready. She put her hand instinctively on her taut abdomen, wondering when she would begin to show.

The yard was quiet when she arrived. David and Jillian,

the couple in the first apartment, were out. Odile wondered idly where they could be, as they were usually ensconced in their house within a half hour after David got home from work, the newness of their marriage having made them blind to any interest outside of each other. Their shabby little brown dog dozed on their verandah.

David and Jillian's was by far the nicest house in the yard. It had been freshly painted when they moved in, in eggshell blue with white trim. Jillian stayed at home, and seemed quite content to do so. She had fancy furniture on her front porch that she had to take in at night so their dog wouldn't sleep on it. She had a row of milk tins filled with flowering plants laid out along the short narrow wall that ran around the little porch. Jillian opened her windows wide every morning, letting bright cotton curtains flutter in the breeze. She swept the tamarind leaves from in front of her house each morning with a stiff-bristled broom, and even had a mailbox with her name on it. Next to hers, the other houses in the yard looked dismal.

Odile had often wondered why they called them houses, when they really were just segments of one long, ugly building. She'd long concluded that the use of the term was an effort in their minds to create separateness when there was none, to achieve some sort of privacy, at least mentally. It was good that they tried; privacy was something you hardly ever found here in the yard.

A fast-moving object whizzed past her head, making her duck instinctively. The boy next door ambled up to collect his ball.

"Odile," he panted, and gave her a wide smile. "You want to throw some balls for me?"

She tossed her braids, forgetting that for school she normally tied them securely back. It ruined the effect. To make up for lost impact, she yawned. "I dunno. Maybe. I just came back from studying. I'm a little tired."

"Later?"

"Maybe later. Right now I'm tired." Perversely, she enjoyed his adulation, even though it often grew quite tiresome. She liked being able to push him around, give him instructions, be the one in charge. In his adoration of her he was docile and tractable, willing to do any little task in order to be close to her. He came in useful. She also enjoyed the fact that he was the only person who could give her any competition on the cricket pitch, even though he was three or four years younger than she.

Rory smiled again, taking her deliberate indifference for a promise. He threw the ball into the air and caught it deftly with his left hand. He was an ambidextrous cricketer, a 'two-hand player,' as he called himself. "You will come out before it gets dark?" he prodded "Okay?"

"Yeah, yeah." Odile yawned again. Pest.

The front door was open. "Ma!" she shouted, simply to let her mother know she was there. She went to her room and rid herself of the burden of her books. She peeled off the light blouse and dark skirt of her school uniform, and stood in her underwear before the mirror, staring at the limber body that she inhabited, the trim tautness of it, and stroked her abdomen slowly.

"Odile?" Her mother's voice was soft behind her, and she spun guiltily around.

Myra stood uncertainly in the doorway, her eyes holding Odile's for long, painful moments, and for a terrible wrenching second Odile thought—she *knows!*

"What, Ma?" she asked, her voice under tenuous control. She drew in her stomach and held her mother's eyes with her own steady ones. Her mother looked at her, and began to say something, paused, then asked about her day.

"Fine," Odile said, shrugging.

"Good." Myra nodded. She threw her another uncertain look, and left the room. Outside, Odile could hear the steady rhythmic thump thump thump of the cricket ball being thrown hard against the tamarind tree.

Rory

Rory watched the backs of Odile's legs as she swayed towards her apartment. The area behind her knees was slightly paler than the rest of her legs. He watched until she was gone.

He hoped she would be out again later, to knock a few balls with him. She was a good bowler, fast and hard. He liked to watch her breasts as they bobbed under her shirt when she drew her arm back for the throw.

He was big for fourteen, and powerful, with huge, clumsy limbs that he carried around with a kind of uncertain awe, as though he had gotten up one morning and—there they were. His face, an embarrassment to him, was covered with a generous sprinkling of acne. White pustules stood starkly out against the blackness of his skin, screaming attention to themselves. He scrubbed at them, washed them in green tea and herbs and store-bought soaps, and yet the pimples grew worse and worse. He was glad that Odile didn't seem to notice them.

He threw the ball against the wide trunk of the tamarind tree, and the tree threw the ball right back. After a while, he took a break, and set the ball down in the crotch of the tree where he could find it when Odile came out.

He strolled across to his porch, where his pet chicken was sitting, watching him disinterestedly. Her name was Gracie. He loved her for her quietness. She never demanded, never complained. She simply existed. He admired that in her, saw it as a kind of strength. Gracie went wherever he did, except to school, of course. He picked her up and clucked softly to her, cradling her in his arms like a cat.

"Chick, chick," he said to her. The chicken looked pleased at the attention.

She had been one of a brood that his father had been rearing for meat, but for some obscure reason, Rory had taken a special liking to this one, and had begun screaming insanely when his father had suggested slaughtering it. Gracie now knew the sound of his voice, and followed him wherever he went in the house and the yard. The chicken could 'heel' like a dog.

It was his greatest fear that one day she would wander out of the enclosure and end up in someone else's stewing pot, so he warned her severely about the dangers of straying. Rory was convinced that she understood.

Her greatest natural enemy was the dog next door, at David and Jillian's place. The animal filled its more boring moments by chasing the poor creature round the yard, much to Rory's horror, and everyone else's amusement.

Rory sat cradling the chicken on the low wall that surrounded the porch, where he could get a good look at Odile when she came out to play. He hoped she would be wearing shorts.

A bright flash of lime green pulled up outside the gate, and the air was suddenly vibrating with the sound of a loud dub music emanating from the car's woofers. The door slammed, and quick decisive footsteps could be heard along the pavement.

The gate at the entrance to the yard creaked. He turned and saw the man that came by to Odile's old lady every now and then: Slim. Rory perked up a bit—Slim always brought with him an aura of excitement. He was a man who was doing things. He was making money selling fake jewelry on the Port of Spain streets, enough to buy lots of real jewelry for himself, to buy all the latest gear and the hottest shoes, and to keep his car looking so cool. He boasted about the chicks in town, how they couldn't get enough of him. Rory worshipped him.

The tall, thin, high-yellow man walked into the yard, not closing the gate behind him. Rory loved the way Slim looked, not black and ugly like him, but nice and light, with bright reddish hair, and no acne.

Rory smiled as Slim swaggered past, cigarette held lightly between finger and thumb, and noticed that he had added a new gold chain to his collection, a really thick one with a cross on it. Rory smiled harder as he approached, hoping he would look down and say 'Good evening,' or smile at least. In his anxiety, he clutched Gracie closer to him, and she squirmed in protest. Slim passed straight by, trailing smoke and cheap perfumed oil. Maybe he didn't see him, so close to the ground.

Slim

Slim pulled up at the curb in a cloud of dust and crunching gravel. His heart was beating in time with the pounding music on the stereo that filled his ears and vibrated in his belly. He eased his long form out of his bright-green ride, and as he did so, admired for the thousandth time the broad stripe of red, gold, and a darker green that ran the length of the car from the front, over the roof, and down to the rear bumper. Idly, he polished a spot with his sleeve.

He was, as his name implied, a slender man, well muscled and toned, with long legs just this side of gangly. His uncertain ancestry had left him with pale yellowish skin and coarse orange hair, but his features were undoubtedly African, lips wide and dense, nose just slightly thinner than those of his darker-skinned brothers, kinky hair twisted into a dozen little plaits that poked out in all directions. He had the overall appearance of a redheaded albino.

He cut the engine but left the music blasting in the car and turned to go inside. Eventually the people next door would complain, but who gave a fuck about them? He strode inside, throwing the gate wide, past the mangy dog, which was on its toes, barking frantically, past the little jackass with the chicken, right up to Myra's door, and threw it open without knocking.

The living room was empty. He made his way to the kitchen,

his next best bet. The senile old fool was there, trying his best to get a few spoonsful of corn soup into his mouth, and failing. The old man didn't look up. Slim eyed him with disgust, watching as he patiently tipped the thick soup down the front of his shirt. Myra should really do something about him.

"Myraaaa!" he bawled, tilting his head back. Where the fuck was she, and why wasn't she in the kitchen? "Myra! It's me!"

Myra came scuttling down the corridor. She was wearing a richly patterned polyester kimono-type wrap that was open at the front to reveal a tight lycra thing that showed the outline of her crotch and the dense form of her thighs. Slim licked his lips.

She stood there, staring at him with this look on her face, like he was a foreigner or something. A muscle in his jaw leapt. He hoped she wasn't going to start up with any talk about how long it had been since he passed by, blah, blah, blah. He leaned against the wall, waiting for his cue.

She stood in the doorway, still staring at him. "What?" he asked in exasperation. "What's your problem?"

Myra turned her dark eyes on his face for long moments, then shook her head. "Nothing," she said finally. She crossed the floor and reached up to kiss him. Her lips brushed his orange mustache lightly, and pulled away, but he pulled her closer.

"That's all you going to give me?" he crooned seductively, and wound his arms around her back, grasping her sweet full ass firmly. He let his long tongue slide around the outline of her lips, then meander towards her ear. She quivered softly within his embrace. He had her now.

"Nice to see you, baby," he whispered. "You smell so good." She laughed softly and pulled away. Her eyes were shining, but there was something else there, something he had not seen before. He squinted at her. "Something wrong?" he asked again.

"Nothing, Slim." Myra's voice rose like a child's. "Why?"

"You just looking a little strange. That's all."

She shook her head and turned her back to him, shifting pans on the stove. "No, I'm fine. You hungry?"

"You know I'm always hungry when I come to see you. Why you bother to ask? What you cooking for me tonight?" He eased his long form into a chair and placed his folded arms on the tabletop. The nasty old man was still slurping away at his soup. Slim shifted slightly, trying to block him out. He could do without losing his appetite tonight.

Myra set a plate before him and began to unwrap bakes that she had in a small pile on the table. "I have some soup," she told him, "and a few bakes. Bakes and accra, and bakes and cheese. What you want?"

Slim was exasperated. "That's it? You mean to say that your man come to see you, and all you can offer him is bake?"

Myra held her hands out to him in protest. "It was left over from today, Slim. I didn't sell it."

"Exactly. You mean all you have to offer me is leftovers?"

"You want me to leave it to spoil?"

"What I want is for you to treat me special every once in a while."

"You don't call, you don't say anything, you just walk in here after two weeks, and you want me to have dinner waiting for you?" She lifted her chin, and gave him a look that made him decide to back down at once.

He reached out across the table and patted her on the hand. "Baby," he said in his most wheedling tone. "Baby, just give me the food. It's all right. We will eat something special another day." It worked. She smiled and rose to her feet.

"You want me to heat up the soup for you?"

Slim glanced involuntarily across at Sebastian, then forced himself to focus on Myra. "Yeah, baby. Do that."

She busied herself at the stove, shifting her pots about and humming softly.

Slim heard a sound behind him and turned in time to see Odile stop short at the kitchen door as she noticed he was there. He smiled at her, flashing long teeth. She had her mother's walk, and Slim often wondered if Myra knew exactly what kind of animal she was harboring under her roof. She was a great-looking piece of young ass, that was for sure. He'd told her once that he wanted to just put her in a brown paper bag and leave her in the back of the kitchen cupboard to ripen, and she'd told him to get the fuck out of her face. The obscenity on her young lips had excited him.

Now she was glowering at him, obviously not expecting to find him here, and obviously not pleased at the discovery. "Hello, baby," he murmured. She shot him a cold, furious look.

Her eyes studiously avoided him. "Ma," she said, like she just made up her mind, "I'm going outside to throw some balls with Rory." Odile turned and stomped off before her mother could answer. Slim smiled to himself and watched her recede.

Myra laid the steaming bowl before him and sat down.

"You not eating?" he asked. He looked at her curiously. Myra had a notorious appetite.

She shook her head. "Nah. I'm not really hungry." Her hand slid to her belly for a second, then resumed hastily to the tabletop.

"You have a belly ache?" His sharp pale eyes didn't miss the gesture.

"Of course not," Myra said. "I'm just . . ." She stopped, and waved her hand helplessly.

"Eat, woman."

Myra got up and served herself. You just had to keep them under control.

They ate quietly and quickly, Slim making sure that he communicated to Myra, in gesture and in tone, just what kind of night he had in store for her. When Sebastian got up and ambled off, Slim moved over to the other side of the table and pulled Myra to him. He slid his hands down her ass and groped it, like large, firm fruit. His tongue flicked out at her, threatening and promising. He knew she liked that.

"You in the mood, baby?"

He felt her quiver under his hands, a slight squirm that he knew she sought to rein in, so unwilling was she to let him have the satisfaction of being in control. He squeezed more persuasively.

"Yes, Slim," she said, voice low. "I'm in the mood."

In spite of himself, he loved the softness and vulnerability of her. When she sat in his lap like this, she went limp, snuggling against him like a little girl, making him feel protective, almost fatherly. He liked the way her thick lashes cast shadows on her cheeks, like moths. He touched her high cheekbone lightly, with one finger.

"Come inside," he urged her.

She protested, even though he knew she wanted to as much as he did. "It isn't even night yet," she said, but she let him stroke the other cheek.

"No matter. That don't matter." He held his mouth very close to her ear. He could tell by the suppleness of her body that she was giving in.

He led her quickly down the corridor to her room and kicked the door shut. They could hear the shouts of the children playing cricket in the yard, on the other side of the wall, but he didn't care. It would be light outside for at least another half hour, and the kids would play until then. There was plenty of time. And besides, if the girl were to come back in early, who the hell cared?

may

Sebastian

May was getting drier and drier every day. Swirling dust devils raced each other up the street, taking with them clouds of dry leaves, twigs, and bits of trash. A wavy haze rose from the surface of the road, undulating above the pitch, making it look like the road was flecked with puddles of dark water.

Sebastian stood at the curb, patiently directing traffic. He windmilled his stick arms about him as cars approached, signaling a halt, then guiding them benevolently along.

"Move along, move along," he instructed with just the right amount of firmness. "Come along, now," he said, moving to the centre of the road, "keep it moving."

Motorists cursed loudly and avoided him in huge, screeching arcs. Sweat was causing his pebble glasses to slide down his slick nose, and from time to time he had to pause from his duties to push them up again.

His pram was parked securely in the shade of the yard's enclosure, propped up under the dusty overhang of the morning glory which draped the fence. Huge lapis lazuli flowers bobbed in the soft breeze. Every once in a while, as though knowing what a pleasant surprise it would be for Sebastian, a flower would detach itself from the vine and tumble into the pram to lie among his treasures.

"Keep it flowing, keep it flowing," Sebastian intoned as the cars whizzed by him. A thin line of sweat ran down his curved back.

Jacob and Myra

They'd gone thirty-five days without rain, the weatherman said, and there were quite a few more to come before the rains got there. The valley was veiled with a sheet of gray dust and smoke that hung like a curtain from the sky, obscuring the hills. Huge clouds of dust, blown all the way across the Atlantic from the Sahara, shrouded the city and lent their magic to the sunsets, causing magnificent light shows of fuchsia, orange, and purple each evening.

" 'Smoke went up from His nostrils, and devouring fire from His mouth' . . ." Jacob read. Psalm 18 was glued securely above the high lintel of his front door; he read those pages standing on a chair. It pleased him to come across a page that seemed immediately relevant to anything in his life. These days he searched the pages on his walls for passages about fire and drought as others read the weather sections of the newspapers.

Jacob enjoyed this dryness in a perverse way: grieving silently for the forests that stood parched and dying, and cursing inwardly as he watched acre after acre of hillside destroyed by the indiscriminate seasonal brush fires, yet somehow in awe of the somber pompous majesty of it all. He enjoyed Nature's showboating, her declaration of supremacy and power as she allowed herself to be immolated each year by carelessly tossed cigarettes and wayward sparks, only to rise again with the onset of the rains. Then, he knew, she would seek her revenge, pouring herself out in torrents and overflowing the water courses, streaming past the fire-raped hills which, denuded, could do nothing to hold her back. He thrilled to the awesome triumph that would occur when she once again declared her sovereignty.

He sat on the porch with a large saddle in his hands, polishing it carefully, admiring his work. Above his head, a wooden sign declared *"Get You're Leather Work Done Here"*, and below it, as an afterthought, the words *"reasonable rates"* were squeezed in in a smaller hand. He had made the sign himself, as he had cut, planed, and assembled his rough work bench and the chair upon which he sat. Jacob believed that a man's home should be a part of him, made by him, by his own hands. And although his woodworking skills were just passable, he used his furniture with pride.

Beside him, his long mahogany *bois* lay on the floor. Although his damaged leg allowed him to walk without the aid of a stick for short periods, he still kept it close, as though drawing from it the residual power of the many prayers and incantations for victory that it had been imbued with all those years ago by the *obeah* women of Sangre Grande. From time to time, he would nudge it gently with a bare foot, and then, reassured, resume his work.

From where he sat he could glimpse the frail form of Sebastian through the vines that clung to the sagging chicken-wire fence. Most of the children were in school by now, as it was after nine, but he supposed that Sebastian would still find lots of cars to assist down on the corner. He shook his head. It was good, he reminded himself, that he was able to keep an eye on him from his work station on the porch, because, although he knew he would be of little help if the old man were to run afoul of the fast-moving traffic out there, he felt comforted to know that he was there, at least, just watching.

"What little good *that* is," he mumbled to himself.

He heard the sharp, bright sound of laughter in the yard and looked up. Myra was coming into the backyard through her rear door, balancing a huge blue plastic washbasket on her dark head. She was calling out to Jillian, the girl in the first house, who was already out hanging up her first batch of washing.

Jillian was a soft brown girl with flesh that billowed up out of her clothes like risen dough. Jacob enjoyed watching her as she moved around the back of the house. She seemed to enjoy being outdoors, and made any excuse to be there: like taking her peas out back to shell them perched on the stairs, or sitting outdoors when her hair was wet, letting it dry in the sun before spending large amounts of time greasing, brushing, and plaiting it. Often he saw her hold up her left hand and admire her wedding ring as it glinted in the sun. There was a softness and innocence and normalcy about her life that Jacob found disturbingly elusive. She seemed content just to be.

Myra, on the other hand, fascinated him because of her dark, brooding face and the complexity of her life. She seemed to be a woman who urgently wanted to have things under control, but who liked earning her own living and being master of her own house. On evenings he watched her step out of the taxi that brought her up from town. She always walked into the yard with her straw baskets grasped in each hand, displaying them as the tools of her trade. Jacob thought she held those baskets as a doctor would a bag of medicine, or a lawyer a briefcase.

Yet in spite of the pride with which she bore her burdens, he knew she was restless and wanted to enjoy her youth. He wondered what she would have been like if she hadn't had the responsibility of caring for a father and a daughter. She looked like the kind of woman who yearned for a freedom beyond the containment of the yard. Sometimes he watched her stand on the front porch and look past the tamarind tree into the street. She stood there with her hands on her hips and her chin raised, and Jacob got the impression she was enjoying visions of herself stepping down the few low steps from her porch, walking the length of the apartments to the sagging gate, and stepping out into the road, never to look back.

He felt that she was seeing in the foggy distance a time when her step out that gate would be her last. The impatient vibrations of her spirit were to Jacob like a musical note, fine and high, carried towards him on the wind. With the painful throb in his thigh and the quiet obedient staff lying at his feet like a Labrador, his own spirit would answer with a similar note.

"Jillian—oooyyy!" Myra called in greeting.

"Morning!" Jillian responded cheerily. She was partially hidden from Jacob's view by the large bedsheet that she was hanging. "I see we get water today!"

"Yes, girl. It's a blessing, with all this heat, and days passing and no water in the pipes. I don't know what's happening to us here. I don't know at all." She set her wash basket down under her own clothesline and began rooting throughout the basket of damp washing, presumably for her clothespins.

Myra's thick hair was wound up in a bright towel, and she was wearing some sort of satiny dressing gown, Chinese-style, as far as Jacob could see, with a broad sash holding it together, and peppered with huge roses the colour of heart's blood, scattered wantonly against a black background. Her feet were thrust into a pair of brown leather sandals; the strap on one had burst, and was dragging in the dust. Jacob wondered idly for a moment if he should offer to fix it for her, then dismissed the thought. He barely knew her well enough to say good morning, after all, and could hardly expect to just waltz up to her—hobble up to her, he corrected himself wryly—and offer to fix her sandal. He abandoned the thought.

Yet he watched intently, fascinated by the sandal strap, dragging behind her in the dirt, and even more fascinated by the curve of her leg, and the prominent knob of bone that protruded at the ankle, causing the overall image of delicacy to tend more to one of solidity and strength. Like a horse, he thought. She had legs like a horse, beautiful but strong. He sat and watched, stroking the smooth saddle in his rough stickfighter's hands.

A white blur flashed past her, squawking frantically, pursued by a brown blur. Myra took no notice. Jillian's dog often relieved his boredom by chasing the boy's fat white chicken around the yard. The animal meant it no harm, but seemed to enjoy throwing the stupid bird into a panic.

Jacob returned to his work, listening with one ear to the muted chat and laughter that came from the women in the yard. Then he was lost in his work again, rubbing at the leather surface that already gleamed as only fine leather can.

He sensed a presence and looked up; with a jolt he recognised the bright red roses of Myra's dressing gown, and his hands fell still.

"Mistress Cole," he said politely, and his mind ran wildly around in circles for fear that he might be expected to say anything more.

"Morning," she said. She folded her arms across her chest, as though suddenly aware that she was standing before him in little more than a nightgown, in the brilliant streaming sunlight. "Hot, eh?"

Jacob nodded mutely.

"I hear we shouldn't expect rain for a while."

"Yes."

"And the brush fires. You seeing all those fires?"

"Doing a lot of damage. When the rain comes, you can imagine the flooding." He eyed her, and looked back down to his work. Their conversations since his arrival had been few and monosyllabic, and the fault lay entirely with him and his preference for his own company. This was the longest conversation that they had had, and, having exhausted the topic, he was once again at a loss for words.

She shifted and hemmed softly. "You fix shoes and things?" she asked eventually, craning her neck backwards to stare up at this hand-lettered sign as though she were seeing it for the first time. "Sandal straps or so?"

Jacob felt better. He was on familiar ground. "Yes. Anything you want. Any kind of shoe." He looked down again at the offending sandal. "You want me to put a nail in that for you?"

She smiled gratefully, and nodded. "Yes. This thing really

giving me trouble. And it's a new shoe, too. From Caracas. I only wore it three, four times, and just look at it." She stuck her foot forward for his inspection. He looked again at the small knob of bone in her ankle. Like a horse.

He nodded encouragingly. "It's not a problem. I can do it for you right now, if you like." He held his hand out, but she stood there, arms still folded across her chest, as though painfully aware of her state of undress and unwilling to enter the porch in that condition.

Jacob rose clumsily to his feet and shuffled forward, embarrassed at his slowness. He took the proffered sandal and made his way back, plopping gratefully into his seat, which offered him refuge from his infirmity. Seated, he seemed quite whole.

He peered carefully at the sandal. It was a pretty shoe, hand-tooled out of rough, uncured leather, but the workmanship was shoddy, and the shoemaker had been careless. He selected a tiny shoemaker's nail from the shallow plastic margarine dish on the table and hammered it securely into place, then put in two more, just to make sure. He was aware of Myra standing on tiptoes at the porch gate, curious.

"There," he said. "There now. It's fine." He eased out of the chair once again, and returned the sandal. She took it and examined it carefully, seeming pleased, and bent forward to slip it back onto her foot. As she did so, he caught a brief view down the front of her gown. Confused, he drew back.

She straightened up with a smile, then her brow furrowed for a moment as she saw the look of discomfort that crossed his face. She gave him a puzzled look.

He was embarrassed; he who had at one time or other sampled almost every young woman in Grande was flushing at the sight of an unconsciously revealed breast. The thought made him feel old.

"How much?" she asked him. "How much I have for you?"

He waved away her question gruffly. "Don't worry," he snapped, and turned before she could protest. Slowly, he walked into the house, leaving her standing there, bewildered.

Myra and Slim

She really ought to tell him. Why had she let all this time slip away with nothing said? She remembered with embarrassment the last time Slim had visited, how just hours before his arrival she had been adamant that this time she would tell him that she was carrying his child. Of course, he'd turned up without notice, like a thief, and, characteristically, she had let herself be swayed by his crude talk, the excitement of him, and his brash advances, and after their heated entanglement she'd been unable to find the courage to speak. He'd wandered off again before morning, leaving a heavy copper bracelet on the headboard of her bed, no doubt a piece of the job-lot of jewelry that he was currently hawking in Port of Spain.

That was weeks ago. She was already beginning her second trimester, deeply aware of the life forming within her, feeling the difference in her breasts and in her appetite. The sensations threw her back a full eighteen years, to that awful period when she was young and stupid and pregnant by the skylarking youngster who'd wanted nothing to do with the whole affair. This time, her uncertainty was no less real, and her fears as to Slim's reaction no less valid.

Why was it that she kept being attracted to the kind of man she knew she couldn't depend upon? Why did she lust after these dangerous, worthless young rebels who lived on the fringe, offering nights of heady carnality without substance? She knew what her friends said about him, and what her neighbours thought. She wasn't blind. She knew Slim for what he was, but that was only half of the story. She knew, too, the heights to which he could take her, and the salacious utterances that made her giddy, and made her feel beautiful and alive and wondrously free. The freedom from the burdens of sanity and common sense was what drew her to him, again and again, and the little voice that reminded her of the insubstantiality of their union was forcibly silenced.

This time, though, she was taking the initiative. She put her clothes basket away and went inside to change. Carefully, she dressed, more carefully than she would have if she were merely going down to the lunch counter. She bathed for the second time this morning, and rubbed her skin down with cocoa butter. She put on a clean brown dress, demure, with long sleeves and a simple straight collar. She put on the same sandals that she had been wearing in the yard, as she knew that she'd be grateful for the comfort of low heels if she were going searching through the streets of Port of Spain for her itinerant lover. The leathersmith, that Jacob, had done a good job.

She left the apartment open, in case her father happened to meander back into the house in her absence, and called out to Jillian as she shut the gate behind her, asking her to keep an eye on things. Her father was standing on the curb, idle for once, hands hanging at his sides. He was staring up the valley at the broad swathes that the brush fires were cutting in the grass.

She placed a hand gently on his shoulder. "Daddy, I'm leaving now."

"Right, right," he answered amiably, not taking his eyes away from the burning hillside.

"You take care," she said.

Sebastian nodded vaguely.

In Port of Spain, the dusty capital city, the traffic seldom abates. Today, the midmorning streets were thick with taxis

and delivery vans, shoppers, hawkers, pickpockets, and beg-
gars. Myra wove her way through the throng, holding her
bag close to her chest, unconsciously twisting this way and
that to shield her belly from arms and elbows, even though
it was still almost as flat as it always was. She chose to look
for him on Frederick Street first; it was the city's major artery,
and she expected that Slim would find sales better there than
elsewhere.

She traversed the length of the strip between Duke Street
and Independence Square without a glimpse of him, and
moved quickly to Henry Street, her next best bet.

He was there, leaning nonchalantly against the open doorway of a little mall, a hand-rolled hemp cigarette clenched
between his teeth. A wooden display case stood propped up
beside him, hung with the gaudy baubles that he pressed
insistently on young passersby. From time to time he turned
to speak to a young man who was selling bootleg audiotapes
from a tray placed upon a high stool.

Myra watched him from across the road for a few moments,
taking in the cocky toss of his fair head and the expansive
gestures that he made as he spoke, wondering what escapade
he could possibly be recounting to his audience of one. Myra
had no illusions as to his fidelity.

He flicked his ash carelessly into the wind, and took another
long drag on the little stub that he held between finger and
thumb. She screwed up her courage and crossed the street.

"Baby!" Slim yelled as he spotted her. He gave his
neighbour a broad grin and caught hold of Myra's wrist.
"Sweet thing, how you doing?" He gave her a wet, firm kiss,
more for the sake of showmanship than for anything else.
Myra could taste the hemp on his lips.

He squeezed her to him and smiled ostentatiously at the
young man next to him. The man ogled shamelessly. Myra
pried herself away and turned to face him, blocking the vendor
from view.

"Slim, you haven't passed in weeks," she began.

He rolled his eyes. "Oh, God, baby, don't start with that. You come all the way down here to start with that?"

She shook her head. "No. I didn't come to start anything. I need to see you. I need to talk to you. How come you haven't passed?"

He gave her one of his wide grins, a grin for the masses, his salesman's grin. "I was busy, baby. I'm a businessman. I was busy. What you want?"

She hated him when he thought he could turn that shit-eating grin on her, like she was some schoolgirl he was trying to dupe into buying some shoddy little trinket, or talk into bed. She spoke firmly and softly. "I just need to see you. I want you to pass this evening."

He drew back his head arrogantly. "You *want* me to pass this evening? You *telling* me to pass?" Then, softly, "What's the matter, hmm? You missing me? You need a little sweetness?" His hand dropped posessively to her waist.

She pulled away in frustration. "No, Slim, I want to see you. That's all. I want to talk to you. You coming, or you not coming?"

The little orange pigtails that stuck out all over his head seemed to bristle with indignant electricity. "You want to talk? Talk now."

She shook her head. "No, I want to talk to you at home. Tell me you'll come this evening."

"Talk to me now."

"No."

"Look, you want to see me, look me. I'm here. Talk to me now. Tell me what it is." His voice was becoming louder.

Myra looked around, embarrassed. The young music vendor had returned to his tray, but Myra knew he was listening. The throng in the streets took no notice, and yet she was convinced that she was on display, a live streetside soap opera.

"Tell me," he said again, and his grip on her arm tightened.

"I'm having a baby," she whispered finally. She didn't know where to look.

"You what?"

"I'm having a baby. You heard me."

He let her go so suddenly, she stumbled. "Whose baby that is?" He stood back and scowled at her. "Whose?"

She looked at him, mouth agape. "What you mean?"

"I'm asking you whose it is, because I know it ain't mine."

Her ears rang, a high-pitched pinging sound, the sound of blood rushing to her head and into her face. "Slim, what you saying? What you talking about?"

"It can't be mine."

"Why not?"

"Because I say so."

She held her empty hands out before her in protest. "Slim," she began.

"I think," he said loudly, gathering up his display case and turning to leave, "I think you better go and look for your child's father, and leave me alone." He was playing as to an audience, words cracking out of him like whips. He snapped his display case shut, and without another word was striding up Henry Street.

Myra stood on the pavement, bewildered and embarrassed. A few passersby turned their heads towards her in amusement at Slim's parting shot. The young tape vendor was grinning, delighted at the little show. Myra turned and elbowed her way through the pedestrian traffic, and headed off to find a taxi to St. Ann's.

Rory

When would Odile be home? He sat on the porch with Gracie in his arms, eyes trained on the gate. The chicken fluffed her feathers and pressed into him, enjoying the rhythmic stroking of his big hands. These days Odile was coming in later and later, with all that studying she was doing for her A Levels. She came in each evening looking tired, with her stack of books clasped to her chest, and each evening he asked her whether she would come out to play a little, throw a few balls for him. Sometimes she said yes, and then he would have a few wonderful moments with her, admiring her skill at the game and her strength and grace as she bowled.

Lately, though she came out less and less, telling him she was tired and that she had to lie down. He didn't like how she was looking, drawn and thin. He wondered anxiously if she could be ill. Their bedrooms abutted, and at night he could hear her turn restlessly through the thin adjoining walls of their apartment. When she did sleep, she moaned often, and cried out softly, words that he strained to make out but couldn't. He sat facing the gate and held the bird closer to himself, hoping she was okay.

"Move with that damn chicken off the porch," his father snapped irritably behind him. Rory's head spun round. His father was standing in the doorway in an old pair of navy shorts and a sleeveless undershirt. He was a huge man, as

Rory would be once he was done growing. Thick wads of gray hair curled up above the neckline of the shirt. He was standing with a beer in his hand, scowling. "Get it off the porch. How many times I have to tell you to get it off the porch?"

Rory got up quickly in case his father was contemplating landing a blow on the back of his head. He was a man with a vicious and unpredictable temper, a temper which Rory would rather believe he had not inherited.

"You have no consideration for me and my asthma. You know how bad that thing is for my chest? I bet you one day you will come home and find it in a pot on the stove."

Rory had heard this threat before, and each time it terrified him. "No, Pa. I'm moving her. See?"

"Just keep it out of the house." His father turned and strode back inside. Rory watched him go with revulsion and hatred bubbling in his stomach. He could feel the resentment rise up his throat to his mouth, so bitter that he was sure it would rot his teeth. They said that two man-crabs couldn't live in one hole, and the faster Rory grew, the faster their hole got smaller. *One day,* Rory promised himself. One day the man-crabs would confront each other, claw-to-claw. One day.

If only his mother hadn't left them. If only that dumb fat fuck hadn't chased her away like he chased everything away. If only she had taken him when she left instead of leaving him behind like a bag of clothes that was too heavy. *No matter, leave it behind, you can always buy new clothes when you get where you're going.* He often wondered if he wasn't so ugly and stupid, big and black like his father, whether she would have taken him along. No way of telling. She wasn't around to ask, never looked back. Ugly and stupid, he reminded himself.

He resumed his vigil from the centre of the yard, back propped up against the broad trunk of the tamarind tree. It was growing dark, the sky was deeply pink and orange, and the light reflected on the walls and windows around him, coloured spotlights at a show. He basked in the light, and suddenly Odile was there, plodding tiredly across the yard, through the bath of coloured lights, and she was pink and orange, too, a ghost in the twilight.

"Odile," he called softly. She walked right past without looking up.

Odile

The vomiting, the loss of appetite, were wearing her down. She couldn't eat, and fell asleep only because of exhaustion after hours of tormented tossing. Many nights she lay on her back with a small cushion pushed up under her nightgown like a swollen abdomen, telling herself, "This is what it will feel like. This is how I will look." The thought frightened her. It horrified her that she was being invaded by some alien growing thing, some selfish parasite that would occupy her body unbidden until it tore itself free.

She hadn't told Blue, and wasn't going to. He'd waited for her each day outside of school as he usually did. Three times she walked straight past, pretending that she hadn't seen him. On the fourth day, he wasn't there. The next week she heard that he was seen with some bitch from another school. She shrugged off the news. One burden less. Yet his reluctance to pursue her stung. He could at least have put up a fight.

She walked slowly past the boy in the shadows towards her home. There were no lights on inside. Finding it strange, she clicked on the switch in the living room, announced her presence with a dull "Ma! I'm here," and went into the kitchen. Myra was sitting there alone in the dimness, silent. Odile flicked on the light and set down her things.

Her mother's face was drawn, and she was wearing a somber brown dress that didn't suit her at all. It looked like a dress you would wear to a funeral. On the counters behind her, piles of packaged food were neatly arranged, as though they were prepared for sale but had never left the house.

"You didn't get any sales today?" Odile queried, puzzled. This had never happened before. "None at all?"

"I didn't go to work." Myra stared dully ahead.

Odile moved swiftly to her mother's side. "You okay?"

Myra nodded "I'm not feeling too well. It's nothing."

Odile held her gently by the shoulders, and looked her intently in the eye. "You sure?"

"Yes," Myra said. "I'm sure. It could be a cold." She waved her hand to dismiss the conversation. "Change your clothes and go and see about your grandfather's dinner."

"Okay, Ma," Odile said. "As long as you're sure you're all right."

"I'm fine," Myra told her. "Don't worry."

Myra

Odile came back into the kitchen and began puttering about on the stove, getting her grandfather's dinner ready. It shouldn't be that much of a problem, Myra thought. There was food on the counter for fifty people. What a waste. She turned slightly in her chair and watched the girl as she set a large pot of soup back on the stove. Maybe she should take some of it across for the leather-man, to thank him for fixing her sandal, since he hadn't let her pay him. Yes, she'd do that.

Myra made a mental effort to rise, but couldn't. A lethargy seemed to invade her bones, making movement impossible. Her anger, hurt, and humiliation weighed upon her.

I'll take it across to him in a little while, she told herself. I'll just sit here a little longer. She sat, enclosed in her own private area of darkness, idly watching her daughter move about on the periphery of her awareness. The child was looking thin and worn. She wondered for a while if Odile were not overdoing it, with all those late evenings at school and the endless nights of study.

I won't tell her about the baby, Myra decided. Not just yet. Not now. She didn't need to be concerned with it for a while. Her studies were burden enough. Myra retreated into her little dark place.

Presently, her father meandered in. His hat and shoulders were covered with leaves, twigs, and dust. No doubt he had spent most of the afternoon standing under a roadside tree. Carefully, he parked his pram next to the table, sitting where he could keep an eye on it.

"Myra," Sebastian said. Huge owl-eyes focused on her through his thick glasses.

"Dad?" she questioned, raising her head.

Sebastian smiled amiably and rooted through his basket. He fished out a smooth white pebble and handed it to her with a flourish.

Myra took the pebble. It was cold and damp. She knew at once that he'd been down to the river again, hunting for treasures. She sighed in exasperation. "Dad, your feet wet? You went walking in the water?"

Sebastian smiled.

Myra looked at the empty space behind those eyes and wondered where her father was, her real father, not this frail, brittle shell. The father who had been a respected policeman with an erect bearing who used to get up extra early in the morning to polish the buttons on his uniform with baking soda. The father who ruled his home with unquestioned authority, who had hit her full in the face that evening eighteen years ago when she'd confessed her pregnancy. Though he fell in love with Odile when Myra ventured back home with her four years later, he never stepped down from his position that the child's conception had been wrong in the eyes of the Lord, and, more importantly, in his own eyes.

Sebastian's only soft spot had been for his wife, a dark Carib woman with lustrous hair, who never once felt the lash of his tongue. Myra remembered watching him come thundering home on evenings, stung by some injustice at work or some horror that he had seen. He was at his worst then, insisting that the table wasn't laid right or that there was too much salt in the dinner. Her mother would throw herself between them, standing between Myra and her father's verbal slings, and Sebastian would simmer down immediately, soothed by the simple sound of her voice.

She was killed on the road seven years ago, hit by a car

that she'd never seen coming. Her father's end began there. He took to visiting the site of her death, shouting warnings to pedestrians to look out, watch their step. Soon, no road was safe enough, and he discovered his life's mission—to be guardian of the town's curbsides.

Myra watched him as he sat with his hands placed carefully side by side on the plastic tablecloth. He was her second child, she thought. *I've got two children, and look at me now, a third on the way. How will I cope? Where will the money come from? Where will I find the time?*

"Go and change your shoes and socks, Dad," she said firmly. Sebastian smiled. Myra turned to her daughter. "Odile, take your grandfather inside and get him out of those wet shoes."

Odile glared at her, and opened her mouth to protest. *"Now!"* Myra snapped. Odile dropped the soup spoon onto the counter with a petulant clatter and tugged the old man out of the room. The girl's moods were changing faster than the wind changed direction.

Myra returned to her reverie. It seemed a soothing place to be, this dark little corner of her mind. Much more soothing than the bright light of reality.

Loud, crashing music jarred her, and at once she recognised the static-filled racket of Slim's car stereo. A car door slammed, and the front gate was wrenched open, but not shut. Her heart leapt for a moment and she thought, *Oh, he's back, he realises he was wrong, thank God,* and she rose to her feet in expectation, facing the door.

The door exploded inwards and Slim entered like a storm, through the living room and into the kitchen, where they faced each other over the table.

Myra looked at his face, and hope died.

Slim reached into the pocket of his red, gold, and green denim jacket and pulled out a wad of bills. "Here," he said brusquely, and held it out towards her.

She stood there numbly, looking down at the money. It was thick with small bills, tens and twenties. She had no idea how much it could be, a thousand, maybe more. She made no effort to take it from him.

"Here," he said again, and agitated the little bundle impatiently.

"What's that?"

"Money," he said, as though she were stupid.

"What for?"

"Get rid of it. I'll pay for the job."

Myra's mouth hung open in shock. "What?"

"Get rid of it. Here." He shook the money before her again.

Myra held on to the table to steady herself. Could he really be saying this? "You want me to kill it?"

"Get rid of it," he said again.

"You want me to kill your child?"

Slim shook his head like an animal with a fly in his ear, as though he didn't want to hear the words. "I told you already, it isn't mine. I'm just offering to help you out. Take the money."

She couldn't believe he was sticking to this stupid story, this brutish, arrogant denial. "Whose, then?"

Slim shrugged. "I don't know. Anybody's. Not mine." He still had not dropped his arm to his side.

"So, when you think I did this, Slim? Where did I get the time to go and get pregnant? And with who? What other man? And why?"

He shrugged again. "I don't know. You had plenty of time. And it could be anybody. You're always smiling with those men down at the lunch counter. And men always walking in off the street down there." He shrugged again. "It could be anybody."

Her response ripped out of her. "You're confusing me with yourself. Which one of us is always chasing down customers, and bribing them with gifts?" She looked at him as though she was truly seeing him for the first time, his shallow self-worship. She marveled at the stupid denial of the obvious, his willingness to believe anything, as long as it did not implicate him, as long as he remained blameless and free. For the first time, she realised how truly ugly he was. The bile rose in her stomach.

She came round the table to face him, rage making her unsteady. "You listen to me," she said carefully and distinctly. "You just listen. You're right. This child isn't yours. It's mine. Just mine. You ain't have nothing to do with it. It was never yours. It's never going to be yours. So you keep your money, and leave. You just leave. Don't pass by to ask me how I am, don't call to find out how the child is, don't do nothing. If you ever see my child in the street, don't speak to him, don't acknowledge him. Better yet, cross to the other side. This ain't no family of yours."

He looked at her with contempt. Deliberately, he tossed the wad of bills across the few feet of space between them. It broke up in midair, exploding in a shower of little leaves. Then she was shouting at him to get out of her house, out, out, out, to leave her family, and when she looked up, she was standing alone in the little kitchen that was littered with small bills, and her father and daughter were hovering in the doorway looking anxiously at her.

"Ma?" her daughter asked, and took a step forward. She glanced down at the scattered bills and then looked worriedly up at her mother. "Ma?" she said again.

Myra shrugged. "It's nothing." She walked to the table and sat down heavily. "Eat."

The other two sat down. Even Sebastian seemed aware of the tension, and glanced from Myra to Odile with wide fish-eyes. They ate in silence, Myra and Odile barely touching their food, Sebastian pouring most of his down his front.

Eventually, Myra stood and set her half-full plate aside. She moved determinedly across to the counter and began preparing a package of fried bakes. She wrapped four of them in a clean towel and set them down into a small basket. Beside these she placed a bottle of linseed punch and a smaller bottle of hand-squeezed orange juice. She was aware of her daughter's eyes on her back.

"I'm going out for a little," she said stiffly. "Watch your grandfather." She stepped carefully around the scattered bills and left through the front door.

She crossed the short distance between her apartment and Jacob's slowly, wondering what the hell she was doing, and knowing only that if she spent one more minute within the stifling confines of her own home, with the ominous pile of bills on her floor and the anxious eyes of her daughter on her face, she would go mad, begin wailing and never stop.

The dry, brittle grass below her feet crunched with each step that took her away from the house. She stood at the little gate to his porch and clutched her basket, wondering whether to call, feeling foolish, knowing she was intruding. Unwilling to call out for fear of what her voice might sound like after all that yelling, she reached out and rattled the latch on the metal gate. There was no movement within the house. She rattled the latch again, more loudly now, and a shadow appeared at the door.

"Yes?" came the gruff question, and suddenly she was too timid to answer. The shadow moved closer, and Jacob appeared on the porch, squinting into the dark yard. She stood there silently, holding the little basket close to her chest.

"Miss Cole," he said eventually.

She nodded. She remembered her purpose and proffered the basket. "I have some things here. Some bakes and things. You had dinner yet?"

He shook his head gravely, black eyes upon her.

"Well, I have these things," she began again. "I was wondering if you want them." She held them out to him, stretching far forward in an effort to hand them over without stepping any closer.

He took the basket from her curiously and looked inside.

"It's just leftovers," she said hastily.

"They smell good," he said.

She nodded.

"You want to come in?" he asked, as though just remembering his manners.

Myra shook her head, but didn't turn to leave.

"Just for a little while," he coaxed shyly.

"Just for a little," she said, and stepped onto the porch.

Jacob and Myra

She was wearing a light-brown dress with long sleeves. It made her look like a schoolteacher, Jacob thought. Or a nun in street clothes. The thought made him smile a little. Unbidden, he glanced down to her feet, and experienced a flood of pleasure when he realised that she was wearing the sandals he had repaired.

He stood aside to let her enter the room. He was curiously exhilarated; she was the first person to enter his house since he came here. That his first visitor should be a woman as beautiful as she . . . His exhilaration plunged as he saw her stand just within the doorway and look around her, unabashed in her naked curiosity.

For the first time he was aware of the smallness and dinginess of the room. It was little more than a bed-sit, with his steel bed in one corner of the room and two chairs and a table in the other. He saw through her eyes the clothing scattered about, the narrow corridor that led to the kitchen, toilet, and bath. The room was illuminated by an inadequate light bulb that hung by a cord from the ceiling. And, oh, God, those sheets and sheets from the Bible, stuck to the wall with the ugly fish-glue that showed yellow through the pages in places.

He watched her mobile face intently as she turned from wall to wall, mouth half open like a child's, until finally she turned to him with a question in her eyes.

"It was like this when I got here," he assured her gruffly, lest she mistake him for a madman. "I didn't put them up. They were there."

She nodded. She walked closer to the walls and looked intently at the yellowing sheets of paper. "Do you read it?" she asked, curious.

He smiled, relaxing a little. "All the time. Come, look." He led her to the window, and pointed to a page on the left of the window latch. " 'I will lift up mine eyes to the hills,' " he read. " 'From whence cometh my strength? My strength cometh from the Lord, who hath made heaven and earth.' "

Instinctively they looked up through the window and out to the hillside facing them. A broad orange path of fire ran across it.

"Where do the hills draw their strength from, I wonder?" she murmured.

"Some hill-god maybe," Jacob suggested musingly.

"Well," Myra said as she straightened up. "He's not doing a good job of it. He's just standing there and letting them burn."

Jacob wondered for a moment if there was anything he could say at that point, and instead offered her a seat.

"Can we sit outside?" she asked. "It's cooler."

He nodded, and took one of the plain, straight-backed chairs, lifting it onto his powerful shoulders. He still had the strength in his arms, he thought to himself. He shuffled through the doorway, ignoring the nagging ache in his hip, and hating the fact that his gait was far from normal. He glanced sharply at her to see if she was staring at his leg. She was, but averted her eyes at once.

"Here," he said, and set it down next to his workbench. He went inside for a moment and returned with her basket full of food and two glasses. He sat next to her on the bench and began to divide the packets of bakes.

"Oh, no," she held up a hand. "I ate."

"Juice, then," he insisted, embarrassed at the idea that he might have to eat in front of her alone. She nodded, and her gaze resumed to the burning hills. Carefully, he poured out two tumblers of the yellow liquid.

They sat in silence. Jacob took the opportunity to admire the fine strong planes of her face, and the dark childlike eyes that to him seemed disturbed, unfocused. He was acutely aware that she was here more in body than in spirit, and wondered what she was turning over in her mind, and why she had come. He searched for something to say, and found nothing. Her eyes dropped suddenly to the thick *bois* at their feet under the workbench.

"My *bois*," he told her needlessly. "I made it."

She looked interested. "You fight?"

"I could," he said. "I did." He set his drink down and leaned forward, eyes gleaming. "I was a master sticksman, nobody could beat me. They came for miles to see me fight. I used to fill the *gayelle* with blood."

"Yes . . ." she prompted him, and her eyes flickered with light for the first time all evening.

"Yes . . . and the *gayelle,* it was in the forest, up in Sangre Grande, sometimes in Valencia or Matelot or Toco, and the forest was so quiet, you could hear the *bois* go crack, when you hit one against the other, and it used to echo through the trees." He set his food down and began to draw expressive arcs in the air with his hands. "We used to slip into the forest in the dark, with a pig to roast and plenty of *babash,* plenty bush rum, and the men used to dig a pit and roast the pig in it, and young men used to challenge me. And the night, the night wasn't like this, not a city night, a country night, with stars clear across the sky, you could look straight up through the trees and see them. You could pick them out one by one, count them, give them names, the sky was so clear and bright."

He stopped for breath, and she looked at him wildly as though afraid that he was done speaking. "Tell me about the fights," she urged him.

Jacob bent forward and picked up the heavy mahogany shaft. It was just thick enough for him to enclose its circumference in his large hands, and just long enough to be held with hands spread out before him, four feet apart. He stroked it as though it were a part of himself, then handed it over. She weighed it in her hands, running her fingers along the length of it.

"I cracked skulls with that," he told her. "And when I was through with my challengers and they lifted them off the fields, the old *chantwells* sang songs about me and my *bois,* and the women brought me food, the best parts of the pig, and the men that had made money by betting on me shoved bills into my pockets. We drank *babash* by the bottle and looked up at the stars, and wondered what they were trying to tell us . . ."

Myra cradled her cold tumbler with both hands, as though she were warming them. Her eyes had lost the dull, remote look that they had worn when she had entered. Instead she was alert, watching his face and his arms as he demonstrated a blow, how he had knocked someone to the ground like *that* . . .

Jacob began to feel like a *griot,* a storyteller telling tales of village heroes, only this time the hero was himself. He sat there with Myra just across the table from him, eyes wide, listening to him talk about a world that she had never known, a world in which he was a champion and an athlete, not a tired cripple. He became expansive, embroidering his tales as he went on.

He told her about the hot full-moon nights when groups of them went all the way up to the northeast coast by bus, armed with liquor and food, and how they used to cook on the beach and stage mock stick battles using driftwood for *bois.* About the night the police came to make a raid, but stayed for bush rum and curried *agouti,* large russet-haired rodents that populated the forest and whose meat melted on the tongue. He talked about the time he actually thought he had killed a man, how he leaned forward in shock to peer at the fallen stickfighter, only to receive a solid blow to the head when the man leapt to his feet; he was only playing possum. He told her about the time the smell of a man's blood had risen in his nostrils and driven him to madness. He began hitting him and hitting him until only the intervention of the spectators had stopped him. Even now that vision of himself, lost to sanity and driven by the smell of blood and the urge to kill, left him bewildered. It was the only time he had ever lost control.

As he spoke, he listened to the sound of his own voice, realising with shock how seldom he actually heard it. He looked up suddenly and realised that the moon was high in the sky. He hadn't even noticed the time pass.

"I'm keeping you up," he apologised. He didn't want her to go, but felt a little foolish for going on like that. Maybe he was boring her. Maybe she was waiting for a gap in the conversation to cut in and excuse herself. He cursed his runaway tongue.

Myra shook her head vigorously. "No, no. I'm sorry. I didn't mean to stay." She rose hastily; Jacob rose, too. They stood regarding each other solemnly over the rough table. The comfortable peace had been replaced by awkwardness.

"Well," she said finally, and patted her hair.

"Well," he said. He began to gather the dirty things up off the table. "Thank you for dinner." He didn't want to lean on his staff.

She nodded, smoothed down the skirt of her brown dress, turned, and walked out into the dark yard. He stood with the dishes in his hands, watching her until she rounded the corner of the building and disappeared into her house.

Rory and Odile

Rory lay in bed and looked out at the sky through the narrow strip of concrete ventilation blocks that ran along the wall of his room. He could just see the edge of the moon. The room was small, and in the dry May heat he had tossed the bedcovers to the ground. After a while, his shorts joined them.

He lay there now listening to the protesting crickets outside, wondering if they were faring any better than he in this awful smoky heat. He listened to Odile, whom he was sure he could feel tossing and turning on the other side of his bedroom wall. He pressed his ear against the wall; it was surprisingly cool to the touch.

He loved to listen to her small movements, loved the thought that she slept with her body pressed so close to his every night. The idea excited him, and he pressed closer to the cool wall, breath coming in rough bursts. He closed his eyes as he rubbed himself against the sheets, trying to imagine her, with her nightdress sticking to her in the heat. (The nightdress was provided for him by his modest imagination. Even in his own fantasies he couldn't, couldn't bear to envision her in the nude.) He could see in his fantasy the sticky braids tossed about the pillow, clinging to her neck and forehead.

He ceased his furtive self-stimulation abruptly. His father would surely know what he was doing. His father had a way of finding out these things, and then he would cuff him down or worse. His young body burned.

He rose to his feet and walked quickly to the window. It was wide open, yet not a breeze stirred. There would be no relief there. Restlessly, he moved to the bed, sat, rose, and sat again. The moon was now fully visible through the ventilation blocks.

The rustle of footsteps in the dry grass made him return to the window. In the darkness, across the way, he could see a gently swaying figure. As the figure drew nearer he recognised the shape of Odile's mother.

"Gawd," he said to himself in awe. Odile's mother was coming from the cripple's house in the middle of the night. His mind spun with the awesome possibilities. He wondered if she was doing it with him, like she was doing it with Slim. He wondered if Slim knew. He lost sight of her as she moved round to the front of the house and let herself in.

Rory waited half an hour or so, until he was sure that Miss Cole would be asleep, then went to the wall that separated him from Odile. He listened long enough to assure himself that she was still awake.

"Odile," he whispered. There was no answer. He rapped softly on the thin board. "Odile."

He heard her stir. He rapped again, more sharply this time. "Odile!"

"What?" Her muffled voice was mildly irritated.

Now that he had her attention, he wasn't sure what he was going to do. "You awake?" he said, aware of the idiocy of the question.

"Yeah," she said. "What?"

"I'm hot."

"Yeah."

He waited, weighing his chances. "You feel like going outside for a while?" *Make her say yes,* he prayed.

"Why?"

"Because," he shrugged, even though she couldn't see him. "No reason."

There was a short silence, and then she said, "Okay."

He almost jumped with happiness. "Go through the window," he told her. "Don't wake your mother up." He went to his own window and leaned outside. She was already easing herself out through the narrow space.

Once on the ground, they went by silent agreement round the front to the tamarind tree and stood leaning against it, side by side. It was slightly cooler to the front of the house, and as the smallest of breezes touched his skin lightly, Rory realised he was still wearing only his jockeys. The revelation made him at once shy and excited; he hoped fervently that his excitement wouldn't show.

"What you want?" Odile asked him archly.

He knew that she was just bristling, as she always did, to remind him that she was older, to remind him who was boss. He let it pass.

"Nothing." He shrugged. The wind touched him softly again, and he held out his arms to embrace it. "I just couldn't sleep. It's too hot."

She nodded absently.

"What about you?"

"What about me what?" She turned her head sharply towards him.

"You could sleep?" He knew that she couldn't.

She shook her head. "No."

"Why?" he prodded.

She threw him a slanted look. "Same reason as you. Too hot."

He prodded again. "I hear you up at night, you know. I hear you turning, and I know you're awake. Late. What's wrong?"

She gave him a long, heavy-lidded look. Eventually, she shrugged. "I keep missing the bus," she said.

"Bus?"

She smiled. Her teeth gleamed in the weak pale light. "The sleep bus. Every now and then, a sleep bus comes along. If you're relaxed and your mind is clear, then you can take the bus, and you fall asleep. If you have things on your mind, or you haven't showered yet, or it's too hot or something, then you're not ready, and you miss the bus. And sometimes it's hours before another bus comes along." She waved it away dismissively. "Just an idea I have. A game I play. I lie in bed and wait for the bus to come along."

"So why you not ready for the bus every night? What you have on your mind?"

She didn't respond. Instead she looked pointedly at her toes, which were poking up from soft piles of dust and tamarind leaves.

"Work?" he prompted.

"Yeah," she said. "Work."

Rory nodded, and the silence resumed for a while.

"What happened in your mother's house tonight?" he asked eventually.

"What you mean?"

"I mean, I saw Slim come and then I heard your mother bawling at him. And he left the house cursing. He nearly stepped on Gracie. *Nearly.*"

Odile shrugged. "I don't know. Something. She was shouting, but I couldn't make out what she was saying. She just told him to get out. And he threw money at her."

"Money?"

"In her face."

"A lot of money?"

"Seventeen hundred. More than seventeen hundred. I picked it up and put it on the table."

Rory looked at her still profile, blurred by the darkness. "That's a lot of money."

"Yeah."

"You could live for weeks and weeks and weeks off that money."

"Yeah."

"What you think it was for?"

"I dunno."

"She asked him for it?"

"I dunno. No. She don't ask nobody for money. He threw it at her."

"Why?"

Odile looked exasperated.

"Okay, okay," he said hastily, then, slyly, "You know where she was tonight?"

"Jillian?" She shrugged.

Rory shook his head and smiled, the secret was too delicious. "She was across the yard. By the cripple. The old man with the shoes."

Her eyes flew open. "She what?"

"Yeah," he affirmed.

She watched him suspiciously. "You lie."

He held his hands out before him to show his innocence. "Really. I saw her."

"Saw her what?"

"Leave his house. Just now. And walk across the yard."

Odile frowned, pondering on this. "What was she doing there, you think?"

Search me, his face said.

She moved closer to him, her face right up to him, so abruptly that Rory thought in half panic that this was it, at last at last at last she was going to kiss him, but she spoke slowly and threateningly in his ear. "You don't tell anybody about this, you hear me?"

Her breath fanned his cheek and he nodded, in the grip of some perverse excitement.

"Nobody," she continued.

He nodded again.

"Nobody, or it's going to be you and me." She withdrew her head and he stood there, giddy, realising that he was finally taller than she was, wondering idly how she would make good on her threat if he betrayed her. *She's forgotten,* he thought, *she hasn't realised that I'm not a little boy anymore, she thinks I'm still the little boy she used to beat down by the river* . . . But he nodded solemnly.

"Nobody," he assured her.

Odile looked up at the sinking moon. "Time to catch a bus." She walked towards the house, slipping round the side into the shadows. Rory waited until she was out of sight, then turned and focused his attention on the burning hills.

Myra and Sebastian and Odile

The money sat on the counter in a neat pile. Odile had sorted the bills the night before, Myra guessed. The pile of small bills, tens, fives, and singles, had been laid out carefully, face up, coat of arms on each bill in the same direction. She picked it up and held it in her hand, flicking through them quickly, her practised eye putting it all at about sixteen hundred dollars, maybe a little more.

"That's what my child is worth?" she said wonderingly to herself. "That's it?" She stared down at the money, then pressed it to her abdomen. *This is what it would cost to pay a doctor to lay me down and rip a child from my belly. This is what Slim was willing to do to get rid of his problem,* tossing it aside like an irritating thought, wrenching it up and out like weeds in the garden. She shook her head.

She had always known, always admitted to herself, that he was no good. He was a showpiece man, shallow and self-absorbed, good for the sex and the wild weekends of music and drink. He reminded her that she was alive, still a woman who needed attention, not a cook and a waitress and a baby-sitter to an old man who had become a burden.

"And what did you give him?" she asked of herself. She put the money carefully back where she had found it and moved to the kitchen sink. Odile had done the dishes last night and stacked them in the drainer, high, a small tower.

She began scouring away at the clean drain with a handful of steel wool. "What did you give him? Your pussy and your pride. That's what. You let him do what he want, say what he want, see you when he want. You let him chase after all those stupid girls, and you say to yourself, he's a man, that is how they are . . . Now look at yourself."

She turned on the taps and let the thin stream of water trickle into the sink. Dry-season water pressure. She was grateful that there *was* water; she had half expected there not to be any.

She'd find a way. Her money would stretch. She didn't need him to help with the baby. She hadn't needed Odile's father, had she? If half the women in the world needed men around to mind their babies, the world would be in trouble. Still, it grieved her. *Our men have let us down,* she thought. *They've let down their women and they've let down their children.* The streets were full of fatherless children; they stood on the corners and smoked their weed, idle, undisciplined. They fought and stole and killed, thinking that was manhood. They didn't know what manhood was, there was no one around to show them. Myra sighed. All those fatherless children.

"Myra."

She spun round, her back to the sink. Sebastian was standing in the doorway. He was neatly dressed in a clean yellow shirt. She could see the imprint of his ribbed undershirt through the thin cotton. His belt was neatly looped around his thin waist almost twice, the worn gray trousers hung on him as on a rack. His face towel poked out of his back pocket.

"Daddy," she breathed. She hoped the anger and distress did not show on her face. She held out her hand comfortingly, beckoning. "Come, Dad. Come, are you hungry?"

"Myra?" he said again, his voice rising. His eyes strove to focus on her face. He came round the table and stood close to her. Myra was unable to hold his gaze, ashamed of her thoughts of a moment before, of seeing him as a burden. She looked down at the thin hands, finely patterned with wrinkles, cracked glaze on tiles. Standing this close, she could clearly see the thick white circles around the pupils of his eyes, like the rings around some planet.

"Daddy," she began. He was afraid, like a nervous child. Somewhere in the corner of his mind he retained the image of her screaming at Slim, shouting like some madwoman, enraged . . . Had he seen Slim throw the money at her? "I'm okay. It was nothing."

He nodded uncertainly, still concerned. "You want to walk?"

She smiled just a little at that. "No, Daddy, not now. I'll walk later. I'll walk with you when I get back from town today. Okay?"

"You want to cross the road?" he asked softly.

Myra patted his thin hand. "Not now. When I'm ready to leave. I'll call you. You can put me in a taxi."

Sebastian nodded, satisfied.

"Sit down. Time for breakfast." She motioned him to the table.

Sebastian turned, and stopped short as Odile entered the kitchen. He smiled with the pure open smile of a child, glad to see her. Odile ignored him and plopped into the seat.

"Tell your grandfather Good morning!" Myra snapped. She had had enough of Odile's moodiness. Her head hurt; she could feel the throbbing veins at her temples stretched to their limits. She wasn't about to tolerate any of Odile's nastiness today. "Tell him Good morning," she said again.

Odile scowled. Her eyes were rimmed with red, and her thick braids were in disarray. The girl should have been in her school uniform; instead she still wore the T-shirt that she slept in. She glowered at Sebastian, then turned her gaze towards her mother. "Look," she said, "ease me up today, okay?"

For a moment Myra was concerned. "You didn't sleep last night?"

Odile sucked her teeth. "I got more sleep than you."

Myra felt her face go cold, then warm. "What you mean by that?"

"Nothing."

"Not nothing. I asked you a question. What you mean by that?"

Odile glared at her. "What you were doing out so late last night? What you were doing across the yard, by that man?"

Myra was taken aback. She'd forgotten about her visit with Jacob; the bitter taste in her stomach when she woke up and the memory of Slim and his callow assault had driven him out of her mind. Besides, she hadn't realised that Odile had known where she'd been. She felt a guilty flush rise to her face, mixed with swift anger at the accusation in her daughter's voice. "Look, child, I'm a grown woman. This is my house, and I will come and go as I want. It isn't for you to be asking me where I go, and who I see."

"You want to have the whole yard talking about you. . . ."

"What whole yard?"

"You want people to see you wandering across the yard that hour in the morning . . ."

"What people?" Myra was mystified.

"Rory!" She began to drum an agitated tattoo on the plate with a fork.

"Oh, for God's sake!" Myra was too distraught to wonder how Rory had come to know of her whereabouts the night before, or how he had managed to communicate the information to Odile before morning.

"You're always talking about how it's your house, and how you can do what you want, and then you go make all that noise, screaming at Slim like that, for everybody to hear . . ."

"Since when are you so concerned about what other people think?"

Odile went on, uninterrupted. "And you throw about this money . . ."

"*I* threw the money?"

"And you don't care, you just shout like you don't care about other people . . ."

Myra looked at the girl, frightened. Odile was shaking, face hot. Her heavy breasts heaved jerkily under her thin T-shirt. Sebastian sat at the table next to her, eyes moving from face to face. She could see that he was growing more and more distraught, and was sorry he had to see this. She contemplated sending him outside, then dismissed the idea. He was far more likely to get himself into trouble when he was frightened or upset. She moved round the table to him and put a steadying hand on his shoulder. He gave her a puzzled look.

It was time to tell her, Myra decided. She drew a deep, steadying breath.

"We were quarreling," Myra began.

"Yeah?" Odile countered, sarcastically.

"Yeah." She paused, and then pressed on. "I told him something."

"What?" In the flush of her anger Odile looked more like her mother than ever.

"I'm pregnant. I told him I was pregnant."

Odile sat stock-still, frozen in horror. Myra waited for a response, heart thumping. None came.

"Odile?"

The girl sat there, eyes bulging, mouth agape, not moving, not breathing, until after an agonizing time, her breath finally came in a ragged gasp.

"Ma!"

Myra held her hands up. "It happened, Odile." The painful rasps that came from her daughter's throat frightened her. She looked at her sharply. "It just happened, Odile. What do you want me to do about it? It's done."

Odile looked at her with an expression Myra had never seen on the child's face before. *"Ma!"* she moaned.

Myra reached for her, hastening to give comfort, but she eluded her grasp and was on her feet and headed for the door.

"We'll manage," Myra called, pursuing her. "Don't worry, sweetheart. We'll manage. We can handle it."

The girl tugged at the front door. It was locked. She spun round, trapped, as her mother approached. "We don't have much," Myra began again, "but we can take care of one more."

Odile managed to manoeuvre the key into the lock with her slippery hands, and wrenched the door open. "Leave me," she snapped as her mother reached for her. Her long legs cleared the short balcony and were flashing, bare, across the yard. Myra stood and watched as she moved swiftly to the end of the yard, then beyond its confines, in the direction of the river.

She turned and reentered the house. Odile would cool off. She needed a little time. It was obvious that she wouldn't be going to school today. Myra hoped that it wouldn't do too much harm to her studies.

In the kitchen, Sebastian was just where she left him. He had plucked his face towel from his back pocket and was sucking on the end of it, owl-eyes fixed on the doorway.

She passed a hand along his grizzled cheek. "Don't worry, Daddy." She kissed the sparse gray crown of his head. Sebastian sucked on the soft terry cloth and didn't speak.

Odile

Madness, madness. Odile plunged blindly into the yard that in the early morning was already heavy with a dense heat. Past Rory's house. Past Jillian's barking dog. Round the back to the hole in the fence. Out into the short expanse of dense dry brush and down, down to the river. Madness.

The path that led to the river was well worn, the red dirt under her feet was smooth and hard-packed. Her bare feet moved swiftly over the damp stones. As she drew closer, the vegetation became gradually greener and more vital, until springy blades of razor-grass swiped at her bare legs, causing filaments of blood to rise to the surface of her skin. She ignored the mild stinging, and kept on.

Her giddy mind whirled. The wretched parasite that clung to her innards, sucking away at her, feeding on her, lurched in response to the churning of her stomach. She fought the nausea with determination. This time she refused to give in to the persistent sickness that assailed her at the beginning of each day.

Then she was standing in the river itself. Its pathetic trickle reached her ankles, cold in the early morning, and the shock of it made her clench her teeth. Yet she pressed on, ankle deep in the river, down its meandering path like a woman hunted by dogs. Throw them off the scent. Down the river that alternately lurched down small inclines and trickled over the flat, on its way to the foot of the hill.

She came at last to a rock that stood at the far side of the river. It was at one of the river's deepest points, a favourite swimming hole of children in the area; in the rainy season it was deep enough for swimmers to leap into from the surface of the rock. She waded through thigh-deep water to reach it, and clambered on clumsily, her tired limbs leaden from the previous night without sleep.

Mosquitoes buzzed gleefully around as she stirred up the water, rising from the sluggish surface of the river in a dense cloud. She clambered up the granite slab that offered few footholds. Spraddle-legged, she sat with her face in her hands. The worn rock was smooth and cold to her bottom.

Ma was pregnant. By that ugly yellow bastard. For a moment she had a vision of Slim with his thin hips and coarse pale freckled skin covering her mother, and heard again the guttural sounds that came from her mother's bedroom when he visited. Nasty. She was a disgrace. The nausea rose again.

So, he'd done her and she was pregnant. The woman had no shame, she was a *mother,* for God's sake, she should have some decorum, some kind of behaviour. Think about the neighbours.

And how would they feed it? Where would the money come from? They barely had enough as it was. Her mother was up by four every morning kneading flour to make her bakes, squeezing oranges, chopping onions, all to sell four-and five-dollar lunches to labourers and handymen in a little shed at the side of the road. And they barely got by, having to share a house with others, a long shoebox chopped into pieces and parceled out. She hadn't thought about *that* when she was opening up her legs to that yellow man, had she, letting his leavings take root in her like a nasty weed.

And what about *her* baby? She, Odile, was the one who needed the attention. She was the one in trouble. She needed her mother to understand her terror, and comfort her in this time of distress, but now Myra had her own concerns.

If concerned she was. Odile pictured her mother, sautering about with her usual arrogance, belly gross, big for all to see. No shame. Drinking up all the attention like she always did. People would whisper how beautiful she was, how plump and healthy, and her mother would laugh her raucous laugh and toss her thick black hair; no shame.

The ruthless irony of it; her mother had always outshone her. She was always more beautiful, always more graceful. People commented on her mother's beauty first, before they even realised Odile was there. They always said, with something close to awe, "What a beautiful woman that Cole is," and then, as an addendum, "Her daughter is pretty, too." And Myra did it on purpose, dressing a certain way, walking a certain way, liking the way the men looked at her, enjoying the fact that people looked at her first, and didn't notice Odile until long after.

Even in her time of fear and guilt, even in her shame, her mother had done it to her again, stolen her thunder. Even now, in scandal, she'd have all the attention to herself, and Odile would be running in second again. Odile brought her head down to rest on her knees and drew her arms about herself. Tall, brittle bamboo creaked and groaned overhead, but apart from that, the river was silent.

Jacob

He was up at his accustomed time, before dawn. As he always did, he sat on the narrow porch stairs facing east, sitting wrapped in his own peace as the dust-laden sky slowly paled. The single naked bulb overhead was still on; its weak rays illuminated the dark clumsy shapes of his workbench and stool. All around it lay shoes and boots of all descriptions, some fairly new and shiny, many worn and down at the heel, all awaiting his attention.

The clutter around him, usually a source of encouragement and satisfaction (work was work, after all) bothered him now. His porch felt dingy and cramped. He wondered how he was able to navigate the limited floor space without tripping over some errant tool or shoe or bag. He wished now that he had been able to afford a more sophisticated workspace, with shelves and a real bench, one with compartments for his tools . . . and maybe another bench for his customers, so that they could sit like civilised men while they haggled over price.

What did that beautiful woman think last night while she wandered through these sparse rooms? He sat in the quiet of the morning and went over, to the best of his recollection, the visit of the previous night. He thought of the strangely agitated look in her bright eyes when she had arrived; a kind of restlessness seemed to accompany her. He thought, too, of the childlike wonder on her face as he described the moonlight escapades that were such a part of country life. She'd been awed at it, city girl that she was. He smiled at that. He tried to recollect the stories he had told, having a vague sensation that perhaps he had allowed himself to get a little carried away with tales of his own exploits. He hoped he hadn't gone too far.

"Get up and make your tea, man," he said to himself, and though his spirit was quite willing, he remained where he was. He rolled his *bois* contemplatively between his hands. "You think she coming back?" he asked it. It didn't seem to have an answer. Jacob sighed.

The yard was slowly revealed by the growing light. He could now clearly see the outline of the three other apartments that stood across the way from his own little house. The huge old tamarind tree stood close, too close, he thought, leaning into it, long, thick arms outstretched as though protecting it from the onslaught threatened by the sun. It creaked in the slight stirring of breeze.

The front door of the centre apartment opened. Jacob watched as the boy walked out into the dawn, hands cupped before him. His lips moved quickly, but Jacob was unable to hear what he was saying. He deduced that the boy was calling the chicken as it swooped down from its nesting place in the tamarind tree. The boy stooped with his cupped hands outstretched, allowing the bird to peck at the grain, or whatever, in his hands.

Jacob watched him intently. Even at this distance he could see the definition in the muscles on his bare back, and the thickness of his thighs. Jacob realised with shock that in the few months he had lived in the yard the boy had shot up. He was gaining weight and height, rapidly undergoing the transformation from boy to man.

He ran an experienced eye over him, taking in the thickness of his limbs and his obvious strength. He thought to himself that the boy would make one hell of a stickfighter, especially if he began his training now. Idly, he indulged himself in a fantasy wherein he would mentor the boy, and pass on his skill, training and honing that magnificent young body until he had the swiftness, agility, and tensile strength of a true stickman. Then, if he wanted, he could return to Sangre Grande in fine style with his new champion, challenging all comers. His name would once again be on the lips of the country people as he pitted his young stickfighter against the best that they would have to offer, and when victory was his, he would be a *Maître* again, this time a master trainer. The fantasy roused a smile, but quickly fizzled as the door of the boy's home was torn open and the bulk of the boy's father appeared on the porch.

Spitting loud obscenities which Jacob could not help but hear, the man descended upon the surprised boy, and began to berate him for his early-morning visit with the bird. The terrified bird took flight clumsily, making sure it was well out of the way of the huge swooping arms which were certainly going for its neck.

Enraged, the bull of a man fell upon the boy, delivering swift, heavy blows to his back and ears. The boy deflected those that he could, and accepted those that he could not without a sound. Jacob watched in silence, admiring the stoicism on the boy's tightly closed face. He knew with a fighter's instinct that the boy had taken his mind to another place, and that the blows fell onto black skin which had long refused to feel them. He knew, too, that this young boy, this champion waiting to be made, had the ability within him to round upon his assailant with a roar and bring him to the ground without effort, yet chose not to do so.

The man turned and went inside amid a final volley of curses. The boy stood to his feet and dusted himself off with a detachment that both entranced and chilled Joseph. He looked for evidence that the boy had allowed his spirit to return from whatever dark place that he seemed to have sent it for safekeeping. The closed, immobile face made him appear all the more dangerous.

With a flapping of wings, the white chicken returned, and with it, the boy's smile. Human once again, he enfolded the creature in his arms, bringing it to his face, lips moving as he no doubt tried to comfort it. He cradled it as one would an infant, rocking it from side to side, walking up and down the narrow area in front of his own porch.

Jacob heaved himself to his feet. It was fully day now, and time for breakfast. He balanced heavily on the thick staff as he got up off the stairs. When he returned to the small kitchen, he spotted Myra's little wicker basket, standing against the wall where he had left it the night before. He took it up and held it between his big hands, inordinately interested in the rough weave of it. Quick excitement ran through him as he realised that the little object would give him an excuse to speak to her again so soon. He'd just pop in, he told himself, and tell her she'd forgotten it so he'd brought it over. Then she'd invite him in for a moment. Yes, that's how it'd go. He smiled to himself.

He decided not to make the tea after all; if he had his tea and then went across, and she asked him if he had had his tea yet, he couldn't honestly say no, could he? Then she wouldn't exactly want to ask him in for a second cup—what would be the point of that?

With excitement that he hadn't felt in a long time, Jacob dressed. He put on a clean shirt, realised that he was putting it on over a dirty body, and took it off again. He tested the taps, praying for water, and was grateful at the light trickle that greeted him. It was better than nothing.

Out to the back of his little house was a water pipe equipped with a shower head above and a washing tap below. A plastic bucket stood at the ready beside it, full to the brim with an emergency supply, should he ever need it. Jacob bathed carefully in the thin stream of water and shaved in a mirror that hung on a nail on the wall. He usually reserved shaving for weekends. He looped a threadbare towel round his waist and returned to the house.

He splashed his freshly shaven cheeks with bay rum, enjoying the sting, and put his good shirt on once again. He took up the basket, and after careful consideration left his staff propped against the wall.

He was less than halfway across the yard when he began to feel foolish. What was he doing this early morning, dressed up and smelling sweet, courting a woman who didn't need to be courted? His pace slowed and his exhilaration ebbed, so that by the time he arrived at Myra's clean white front door he was contemplating leaving the basket on the low porch and escaping.

Instead, he knocked, more tentatively than he cared to think about. There was no response, so he knocked again and stood away from the door, patient. The door creaked open. Jacob contemplated offering to oil the hinges, but contemptuously dismissed the idea as the urge of an adolescent.

Sebastian peered beyond the door, face twitching nervously.

"Good morning, Mr. Cole," Jacob said as politely as he could.

Sebastian watched him intently, and said nothing.

"Can I talk to Miss Cole?"

"Morning, son." Sebastian said finally. He gave him a watery smile.

"Morning," Jacob said again, and continued to wait. Sebastian simply stared. Presently, Myra appeared in the doorway behind her father.

With mild shock Jacob took in the hair in disarray, and the wild, red-rimmed eyes. He knew with sudden pain that he had chosen a bad time to come. Instinctively, he took one step backwards, almost running afoul of the porch stairs. "Good morning," he managed at last.

Myra nodded vaguely, and watched him uncomfortably, waiting for him to state his purpose.

"You left your basket," he said, proffering it. "I'm just bringing it back. Thank you."

Myra accepted the basket and nodded without speaking.

"Thank you," he said again, and turned hastily to leave.

"I'm putting her in a taxi," Sebastian informed his receding back.

Jacob hurried back to his house, embarrassed. He knew that he had intruded on a private moment, stepped carelessly on some pain that was hers alone, and he cursed himself for it. He cursed himself again as he tore the shirt savagely from his back and tossed it into a corner. *How stupid,* he thought to himself, *how stupid you were to appear there like a boy, with her basket over your arm, stinking of cologne. Stupid of you.*

He moved to his kitchen, tossing things about, and set his small, dented kettle onto the stove to heat water for his tea.

Odile and Rory

"You ain't been to school all last week," Rory told her, settling down next to her on the steps. She sighed. She'd really have preferred a little peace this early morning, but he was making himself comfortable next to her. At the start of the new week, the light-blue shirt and khaki pants of his school uniform were clean and pressed, and he smelt faintly of soap. She wished he'd run off to school and leave her alone.

"Don't think I didn't see you," he continued. "You put your uniform on and then you duck down to the river. I bet you stay there all day."

Odile regarded him with narrowed eyes. "So?"

"So I met some of your friends round the Savannah yesterday, and they're talking of coming up here to see if you're okay. They said you never stayed away from school before, so you must really be sick. I had to tell them not to come, or else your mother would find out." He paused, waiting for her thanks. None came. "Then you'd be in trouble," he added finally.

Odile looked away from him and towards the fence at the far end of the yard. "So? Who cares? What kind of trouble would I be in?"

"Your mother . . ." Rory began again, earnestly.

"To hell with her," Odile ground out with a savagery that

surprised him. "To hell with her, you hear me? I can't get into any trouble with her. What she going to do, spank me?"

Rory watched her warily, unfamiliar with this new Odile who was developing a vicious tongue and a surly disposition. "Y'all fighting or something?"

"No, we're not fighting."

"I don't believe you."

"We're not fighting. We're not even talking."

His eyes widened. "Yeah? Why?"

She sucked her teeth and turned to look at him again. For a moment she wondered if she should say anything. The way it is living in a yard, you breathe something to someone, next thing you know, it's on everyone's tongue. There was no reason why Rory should be any different. On the other hand, she thought, in a month or two when her mother began to show (she couldn't even bear to apply the idea to herself), it would be all over the yard anyway. "She says she's pregnant," she said finally. "That's why." She smirked to herself at this, awaiting his reaction. She was not disappointed.

"Gawd!" the boy said, smacking his forehead. His eyes goggled. "Not really?"

"Really," she confirmed dryly.

"Gawd! Who did it? The cripple round the back?"

"Don't be an ass!" she snapped. "Look, don't get me damn vexed here this morning. What would she be doing with him?"

Rory put his hands up in defense. "I just wondered. Slim, then."

She nodded curtly.

"Gawd," he breathed.

"Stop with that. Stop saying 'Gawd' all the time. You haven't had enough of that 'Gawd' thing?"

Rory was silent. "So he's really gone and done it," he said after a while. There was an unmistakable note of admiration in his voice that caused her stomach to churn. The stupid boy had always been a fan of that yellow bastard. When he was younger, he used to imitate his walk, bumping arrogantly round the yard like a jackass. He even wanted to get a jacket like Slim's, a nasty denim thing in Rasta colours, with pockets everywhere. She was disgusted.

"What you think that makes him, a hero?"

Rory couldn't find an answer.

"Go to school, child," she told him.

He stuck his chest out at that. "Who you calling child?"

"You. Go to school."

He opened his mouth for a moment, and shut it quickly.

"Yeah," he said, and rose to his feet and left.

Odile remained on the steps for a while, then roused herself. Her mother was in the kitchen rolling out the dough for the day, and although she was hungry, she chose not to go in looking for food. It was intolerable to be in the same room with the woman. Myra had tried talking to her for a while, almost pleading with Odile to listen and to understand, but Odile's response had always been to get up and walk out. Eventually, she stopped trying, and now whenever Odile was around, her mother settled for waiting in silence for a word from her. Odile's mouth twisted at that. If she was waiting on some kind of conversation, she had a long wait coming.

She crept into the house and collected her books from the coffee table in the front room. She was already in full school uniform—she had taken to leaving the house as usual, pretending to be on her way to school. Then, as Rory had no doubt observed, she would walk just a little way down the street before ducking down one of the many paths to the river, as soon as she was out of sight of the house.

She balanced the books on her hip and set off out of the yard. She reached for the latch on the front gate but encountered a large, heavy hand instead. She started with surprise. The leather-man from round the back was just unlatching the gate, on his way in.

"Miss Cole," he said politely.

She stared at him balefully as he held the gate open for her, and did not respond.

"How's your mother?" he persisted as she slipped through, carefully avoiding any physical contact with him. The question brought the blood to her head. Who the hell did he think he was, asking about her mother like that? That was Myra for you, always bewitching some nothing man with her swinging hips and loud laugh. His obvious interest sickened her. She slipped past him without responding and, books clutched to her chest, walked swiftly down to the end of the road, where she disappeared behind a clump of dry bushes, turning in the direction of the river.

She peeled off her shoes and socks and, stuffing the socks into her shoes and tying the laces together, she slung the shoes across the back of her neck. The river was cool to her feet. She knew her destination, and moved without hesitation towards her rock. She followed the meandering trickle, stepping carefully to avoid the bits and pieces of sharp stone, glass, or metal that littered it. The thought struck her that soon she would be too large and ungainly to effectively negotiate the river, and she laughed, a short, bitter bark. "Fat as a sow," she muttered. The thought struck her as exceedingly funny.

She rounded the last bend and drew back, startled. She was not the first one to arrive at the rock. Rory sat on its rounded top, barefoot, with the legs of his khaki pants rolled up to the knee. His shoes and books had been carefully placed behind him. He was sitting facing the direction from which he knew she would come.

It wasn't until she was herself seated atop the mound (refusing his proffered hand) that she spoke. "What you doing here?" she asked him aggressively.

He looked at her with a strange, mild, closed-off expression. "I'm keeping you company today," he informed her firmly.

"You what?"

"You heard me."

"I don't want any company. I want to be alone."

"Too bad."

She poked him in the ribs with irritation. "Go away, Rory."

He brought his face so close to hers that she could feel his breath. "Make me," he said simply.

Odile recoiled in shock. Over the years that they had played and fought together, she, as the elder by three years or so, had always been the one in charge. Now this boy was actually defying her. She was stupefied. "What?" she managed at last.

"I said, 'make me.' This is everybody's river. If I want to be here, I can. That's all."

"I'm leaving." She made no effort to move.

"I'll follow you."

"Your father find out, he'll cut your ass."

"You going to tell him?"

Odile gave up, baffled by this new assertiveness that the boy was displaying. What had gotten into him? She sat in silence, trying to pretend that he wasn't even there.

"Odile," he said softly, and reached out for her hand. She was too stunned to pull away. The boy had never had the effrontery to touch her like that before. "You want to talk to me?"

"And say what?" she asked scornfully.

"I dunno. Why you so vexed with your ma?"

"No reason."

"What you mean, 'no reason'? You not even speaking to her. You cutting classes all week. You must have a reason."

Odile sat, thinking of his hand over hers, and the thumb that was gently drawing circles in her palm. It was absurd. "I told you," she said finally. "No reason."

He persisted. "You must have a reason. Things don't just happen so. You afraid when the baby comes she won't have time for you?"

She snorted. "I'm old enough to take care of myself."

"You think y'all can't mind it properly? You worried about money?"

"I don't care. That's her problem."

Rory shook his head.

"You don't understand," Odile told him.

"Help me understand."

"No."

He shook his head sadly and looked away. "You know," he said eventually, "I can tell you a secret." He turned around to face her fully, without letting go of her hand. "Let me tell you something. All those worries, all those things that you're letting bother you, you don't have to feel them. Or see them. Or hear them."

She was puzzled. "Eh?"

"You don't have to let anything bother you if you don't want it to. You can just go to your own universe and lie still until it passes."

"What you talking about, Rory? You gone mad?"

"No, look." He bit his lip hard for a moment, trying to find the words. He took a breath and began. "Everybody has their own universe, okay? It's just like this one, only it's yours and you're in charge, because it's in your head. You can let anything out of it or keep anything inside, and put it anywhere you want to, like moving furniture around in your head. That way, you can make all the big things seem like little things. You can turn red into blue if you want. And nobody can tell you different."

"So what, you just make up a life in your head, like a madman?"

"No, it's the same life you have, only you have control of it, okay? And anything that's bothering you, you just put it out. Anybody you don't like, you just tell them to get out, because it's your universe."

"Suppose they come in again?"

"They can't. Because you put up these walls, okay? Big high walls, and nobody can pass, if you don't want them in."

"Really? And they don't keep trying to get in, all those thoughts and worries and people?"

"Nah. Not if you make the walls high enough. You make it too high and they can't get over, and too wide and all that, like in the song."

"What song?" She furrowed her brow.

He looked exasperated. "The song from Sunday school, about the walls of Jericho. You know, 'Too high, can't get over it, too low, can't get under it, too wide, can't get around it . . .' You know, that song."

Odile knew what happened to the walls of Jericho. "Suppose you put so many things outside your walls that they all start to gang up on you, and push and push on the walls, until everything caves in?"

"Can't happen," Rory said dismissively. "Never happened."

Unconvinced, Odile didn't answer.

They remained in silence, unmoving, watching the mosquitoes hover in droves just above the sluggish surface of the water. Rory didn't take his hand away.

Myra and Jacob

Whenever Odile left for school, Myra felt as though a tremendous build-up had been released within the house; it was like holding a hissing pressure cooker under an open tap. She paused at the counter where she was kneading the morning's dough and pressed her floury hands to her hot face. Her life had become intolerable this past week; the child barely spoke, went straight to her room each day after school, had even ceased to attend to her grandfather. Many evenings Myra had returned from the lunch stall to find Sebastian wandering aimlessly about the yard unfed. Once he'd become so hungry that she found him seated at the table chewing on a slab of cold lard. She'd taken it away from him, crying huge, agonising tears which Sebastian had tried his best to dry with the dishcloth. When she scolded the child about it, she'd received nothing but a cold stare, more full of venom than Myra could have thought possible from her good-natured daughter. She recoiled and withdrew, and now accepted the hateful silence with hurt resignation.

Now the house was quiet, Sebastian was probably out by the gate helping the neighbourhood children down to the end of the street, and she could have peace for a small time. She stood over the pale dough with her face buried in her hands and wondered if it would ever be right again.

The child that was growing inside her—how could Odile

resent it so much? It was not as though Odile was still a baby herself, in need of the kind of attention Myra would have to give it when it came. It wasn't as though they were so badly off, or that the house was crowded. Odile would still have her own room, at least for the first few years.

Of course, she'd made no secret of her hatred for Slim; she'd always said he wasn't to be trusted, that he was a player, and a selfish one at that. Now, with the wisdom of hindsight, Myra supposed the girl had been just a little bit right.

All this, she reasoned, still could not account for the hate that shot out from the child like a fire, aimed at her child and, Myra admitted, at her What had changed? When had her daughter began to turn into the silent, malevolent shadow that she had become?

She realised that someone was knocking at the front door, and had been knocking for quite some time. She shook herself awake and went to open the door. Jacob stood on the porch a few paces away from the doorway. He had obviously been about to leave. He turned tentatively.

"Miss Cole," he began. He tried to avoid leaning on his staff; she tried to avoid looking at it.

"Myra," she corrected automatically, then realised with horror that her face was dredged in flour that had rubbed off from her hands. "God," she said, and her floured hands flew to her cheeks, making it worse. "Excuse me. Wait here." She made a swift and embarrassed trip into the kitchen, splashed water from a storage bowl on to her face, and returned to the porch to find that he had not moved a muscle.

She smiled politely but inquiringly. "Morning, Jacob," she said encouragingly.

He shifted uncomfortably. "Ah," he began, and scratched his ear with a forefinger. "Ah, look, I don't want to be interfering in your business . . ." He faltered, and began again. "I don't want to be interfering in your business, miss, but, you see, I'm a country man, country people believe that raising a child is everybody's business. You follow me?"

Myra nodded, although she didn't.

"Yes, it's everybody's business, you see? And if a man sees a child doing something wrong, it's his business to discipline the child, or to make sure that the child gets better instruction, you see?"

Myra nodded again, curious now.

"And, well, miss . . . you know I saw your daughter leave for school and then duck down by the river?"

Myra was aghast. "When?"

"Just now. This morning. She had on her school uniform and her books, and I bumped into her by the gate. But she ducked down one of the tracks at the bottom of the road, headed towards the river."

"Good Jesus," Myra said. What now? What was her daughter up to? "She never did that before," she said.

"Well," Jacob said as gently as he could, "she did it this morning."

Myra said nothing.

"You think she could just be playing?"

She shook her head. "No. She's not playing. She never played like that. She's a good student. She has her A Levels next year. She wouldn't do that, not for fun."

"I know it's not my place, but she having problems or something?"

Myra shook her head mutely. She knew if she attempted to answer, the tears would humiliate her in front of this kind man.

She searched for a response, and then the shrill call at the end of the yard interrupted her thoughts. "Myra-ooooy girl! Myra-ooooy!" Myra strained to see round Jacob's broad shoulders. He himself turned in the direction of the call.

Jillian was at the gate, rattling it feverishly "Myra girl! Come, come!"

Choking on her own heart, she ran towards the gate, with Jacob moving as quickly as he could behind her. "What? What?" she demanded breathlessly as she caught up to the colourful figure.

"Girl," Jillian gasped, her huge bosom heaving with the

effort. "Your father down in the centre of the road by the Savannah, directing traffic."

Myra didn't stop to ask anything further. She ran to the end of the street, apron flapping at her knees, tugging fiercely at the apron strap around her neck that suddenly seemed too tight. She was aware of Jacob at her side, clumsily keeping stride with her.

"I'll go alone," she told him.

"No," he said. "I'm coming with you."

She didn't try to stop him.

Sebastian

He stood at the busy junction, where the ripples of traffic wound their way down the treacherous Lady Young Road to meet the fast flow of cars pouring down out of the Maraval and St. Ann's valleys, all coming together, flooding together to join the stream that gushed crazily round the huge expanse of land that was the Savannah. The heavy traffic was converging at the junction of this enormous grassy roundabout, coming in from the north and the east, all jostling with one another in their bid to enter the city. Five lanes of traffic squeezed into a roadway built for four, honking, shoving, surging forward. That's why he was needed, to help with this vicious snarl in the road.

Cars nosed at him like sharks, coming at him and then swerving away. Didn't they see his hand signals, for God's sake, didn't they know the rules? And all the noise, horns, and angry voices, impatient young men cursing. If they would just look at him, look at his hands, didn't they know the signals? Didn't they know the rules of the road?

Then this woman comes rushing up at him, running out into the traffic, without his permission, into the stream of cars, like she didn't care if she got hit, running into the road and holding on to him, shaking him. He was doing a job, couldn't she see that, but she was calling him Dad, and saying *Dad, Dad, get out of the road*. It was so funny, this woman, calling him Dad, trying to get him to leave his post, a working man like himself, and this man with a stick was pulling him, too, actually lifting him up and taking him out of the road, in the middle of all that traffic, snarled-up traffic he was supposed to unsnarl. The woman hopped frantically around, saying *Dad, Dad, are you okay.* It was so funny, her with flour in the edges of her hair, shrieking at him. He started laughing.

Jacob and Myra

Jacob eased Sebastian into the taxi with difficulty. His hip shrieked with the effort, and the old man struggled with surprising strength. The wild, hollow laughter chilled him, and he sensed Myra hovering anxiously behind him, felt the tears that she shed as though he were shedding them himself. He put a restraining, comforting hand on the old man's shoulder, and whispered gently to him that he should sit still, and that he was going home.

Finally, with a sigh like air escaping a tire, Sebastian gave in, and the frail, aged body went limp in his arms. He settled into the torn and bedraggled seats of the old taxi, looking like a small boy in his thin khaki pants and pale-blue shirt. The taxi driver looked back, craning his neck to see over the front seat, at the whole proceedings. "He crazy, or what?" the man asked, showing widely spaced yellow teeth. "Eh? He mad?"

Jacob threw him a look that cut him dead. The taxi driver turned to grip his steering wheel and stared straight ahead. "Hurry up," the driver said after a while, "I have work to do."

Myra disappeared for a moment, but returned before he could turn around to see where she had gone. She held in her hands the big old pram, a tangle of wire and fabric. The traffic had done its worst. Her face twisted as she held it out before her, like a child asking her father to fix a toy gone bad. Jacob took it from her, insistently prising it out of her grasp, and forced it into the backseat beside Sebastian.

Myra turned to venture into the fast-moving traffic once again; he stopped her with a firm hand.

"Where are you going?"

She pointed at the scattered debris that had fallen from the old man's baby pram: newspapers, small stones, books, pencils, a crushed doll's head that lay in a macabre tableau across one of the dividing lines in the road. "I have to get his things," she said, trying to twist out of his grasp. "His papers, and his doll and things."

"No, don't go back into the road."

"His things. His papers and things."

"He can collect new things. Don't go into the road again."

"Jacob . . ."

"Get in."

She didn't argue this time, but squeezed in beside her father, with the pram's twisted wreck uncomfortably between them. Jacob heaved himself into the front seat, holding his staff between his knees, and instructed the driver to drive off.

As they drew up at the yard, he was out of the car before she was, and opened the door on Sebastian's side. The old man had quietened by this time, and came out of the car meekly and without complaint. He watched with disinterest as Jacob tugged at the old pram and laid it carefully down on the pavement.

Myra took his hand. "Come, Dad, let's go inside."

"Myra!" He beamed at her in pleasant surprise, as though he was seeing her for the first time today.

"Yes. Let's go inside."

The door was unlocked, as they had left it, and Jacob followed them into the house without hesitation. Eagerly he absorbed as much as he could. It was the first time he was entering it, and there was no guarantee that it wouldn't be his last. He looked curiously around, taking in the clean, flowered curtains, the faded framed print on the wall bearing the Sacred Heart of Jesus. The golden halo that surrounded the heart had deteriorated over the years into a coppery green. The house, he realised, smelled strongly of food and frying, as though years of food preparation had left their fingerprint on her furniture and walls and ceilings. He followed Myra and Sebastian down the corridor and into the tiny bedroom at the back of the house. It was a neat room, painted in cool green and housing a narrow single bed and a large hand-tooled chest of drawers.

She sat her father down on the bed and then looked round to see Jacob staring. Her eyes followed the direction of his gaze. "My father made that for me," she told him, pointing at the chest of drawers. "A long time ago."

"Yes," Sebastian agreed, surprising them both. "Yes, yes." His eyes swam about like goldfish in shot glasses.

"You remember?" she asked him with hopeful surprise. He gave her a vague look and then turned away.

"He remembers," Jacob said, more in an effort to soothe her obvious anguish than because he actually held that belief himself. If Sebastian had indeed remembered, there was no evidence of that on his face right now. Jacob knelt at the bedside and eased Sebastian's shoes off, then coaxed him into stretching out his legs onto the bed. The old man stank with the dank must of age, hair unwashed, the sweat of his recent exertions clinging to him. Jacob wondered for a moment if that rude, lazy granddaughter of his wasn't supposed to be looking after him. What was she busy doing that she couldn't help her mother by making sure the old man had a bath now and then?

"Take some rest, Mr. Cole," he urged him.

Sebastian obediently lay still. They watched him until they were sure that he was drifting off to sleep, then silently left the room.

Crisis over, his role as hero ended, Jacob was uncomfortable once more. He cleared his throat self-consciously and stood in the living room, waiting for a signal that would tell him to stay or go. Unsure, she watched him solemnly.

"Let me make some coffee or something," she suggested at last.

"Yes," he said. "That's fine."

She nodded and preceded him into the kitchen. He stood at the table as she busied herself filling the kettle and setting it onto the fire.

"You can sit, you know. It ain't a courtroom or anything. You don't have to stay on your feet."

He sat gratefully. While she rooted around getting the coffee things together, he eagerly drank in the room around him. The food smells were obviously strongest here: the walls themselves seemed to harbour memories of the many mornings she spent getting her foodstuff ready for sale. Above the stove, the smoke had created wide, blackened circles on the board ceiling. It needed repainting. He held himself back from offering to do the job for her. If that red-nigger with the hair like packing twine, the one that he saw coming in and out of her house from time to time, couldn't do that, well, it wasn't his place to ask why.

She set two huge mugs down onto the table and poured generous helpings of milk and sugar into them. She scooped in heaping spoonsful of powdered coffee and then, to his surprise, brought down a flask of white rum. She held it out to him enquiringly. About to say no, he thought better of letting a lady drink alone, and nodded instead. She splashed two fingers of rum into each mug. The kettle murmured contentedly on the stove.

They sat across from each other at the table, arms folded before them, each one mirroring the other. She looked tired, her shoulders seemed hunched, and there were signs of strain on her handsome dark face.

What could be weighing down this woman, that each time he saw her she seemed to be carrying a larger and larger burden? Should he ask?

"You father doesn't usually do that kind of thing," he prodded. "I mean, he usually stays up here, on this block."

She nodded. "Yeah. He never went that far before. I don't

know how he made it all the way down the hill to the Savannah by himself."

"It's a long walk."

"Yeah."

"Why did he do it?"

"I don't know." Myra took one of the mugs of rum and peered longingly into it. "I could drink this straight, right now," she murmured, "without the coffee."

"Wait until you have the coffee," he said gently. "It's kind of early."

"Not the way I'm feeling."

"How are you feeling?"

"It isn't important."

"Myra, listen." He wondered whether he should say anything. It wasn't, after all, any of his business. But he wanted it to be. He began carefully, trying to make himself understood. "You can't just block people out like that. You can't just sit there and pretend that nothing's going on, because I can see it on your face and hear it in your voice. You have to do something, or talk to somebody. You can't just let things sit inside and poison you."

"I haven't got anybody to talk to." She looked defeated. Jacob ached with the frustrating sensation of being so close and yet not being able to do anything.

"Talk to me," he said simply.

Their eyes locked for an age. A flood of confused thoughts washed across her face as she struggled against her natural reticence and self-reliance. Finally her walls tumbled down, and for the second time today, she was in tears. Yet these were welling up from a deeper source, full of frustration and anguish and hopelessness. Jacob stayed where he was and let her cry, afraid to move towards her or to touch her in case he interrupted the healing flow. He sat silently until she was done crying, and the words began to pour out of her.

"It's just, it's just that it never stops. It never stops. Taking care of Dad, it's like having a child in the house again, and he just doesn't understand, he doesn't know me sometimes, he's always wandering off and I don't know where he is. He's always wandering off, you know? Down by the river or something, or walking in the road. I worry about him so much. What you think it's like for me, working my ass off down at the shop and all the time worrying that when I get home, he'll be missing and then they'll find him at the bottom of the river? And I work so hard, it feels like it's all I do. You think I ever get to go to parties or the cinema or anything? No, because all I do is work and worry about him." She paused for breath.

"What about your daughter? She's old enough to help. Why doesn't she help with the cooking?"

"Oh, she has exams to worry about. She has to study. I wouldn't want to spoil her chances, have her end up like me, selling bakes and juice all her life."

He smiled at that. "There's nothing wrong with selling bakes. But why doesn't she take care of her grandfather? She can take some time off to at least make sure he takes a bath. Or sit with him for a while when she gets home."

"Oh, she used to spend time with him. She just doesn't anymore. She doesn't have time for him anymore."

"So talk to her."

"I can't. She isn't even speaking to me."

Jacob was shocked to the depth of his old-fashioned heart. Where he was from, in the country, there was no such thing as a child not speaking to a parent. The code of respect for elders was too rigid to allow that. "What do you mean, not talking to you? How could she be not talking to you?"

"She hasn't said anything to me all week. She won't even eat if I'm in the kitchen. She won't even look at me."

"Why?"

"I don't know." Guiltily, she tried to avoid his gaze.

"No, tell me." He was conscious of her leg twitching wildly under the table.

"I told her I'm pregnant."

"Oh." He said nothing for a while. What could he say after that?

"Yes, well . . ." She looked embarrassed.

The kettle, with its keen sense of timing, chose that moment to begin shrieking. Glad for a distraction, he hopped to his feet and brought it across to the table and filled the waiting mugs. They sat blowing on the hot drinks as though cooling them down were the most important task in the world.

Finally he spoke again. "So your daughter is upset about that? Why? She doesn't want it?"

Myra shrugged. "She hasn't said anything. She isn't talking."

"What about the father?"

She took a long draught of the too hot drink, swallowing without flinching. "I'm the father."

Jacob had the wisdom to leave it at that. "Okay."

She nodded. "Okay."

They sipped their coffee in silence. The strong white rum burned as it made its way down.

june

Jacob

Jacob pursued Myra the best he knew how. Cursing himself for being such an adolescent, he discovered a thousand ways to meet her by accident. He took to walking out to the corner when he knew she would be back from town so that he could offer a hand with her heavy bundles. He found himself fixing small things around the house, loose wires, unsteady table legs, broken hinges. He made her a waist pouch out of good cured leather and offered it to her to keep her money in when she made her sales. He had put in separate pockets for each denomination of coin, and two big ones for bills, one for her change and another in which to accumulate larger bills for deposit.

"Somebody commissioned it," he lied when she expressed discomfort at accepting what was obviously such a valuable gift. "They never came back for it, and it's been lying around. I can't even get it sold. So I thought maybe you could use it."

She fingered the stiff new pouch and inhaled its freshly cured scent. She knew he was lying; he knew that she knew. But by silent agreement, each pretended that the story had been accepted, and she put it away graciously. In return, she sent him warm fresh bread, soups, and punches as often as she could afford it.

He took upon himself a moral responsibility to keep an

eye on Sebastian. The old man didn't seem inclined to wander down to the Savannah as he had done just a few weeks ago, but did sometimes make it to the river. When he did this, Jacob would sigh, lay down his tools, and set off after him with the martyred patience of a frustrated father. When he recovered the old man and convinced him to come back to the yard with him, he always made sure to let Myra know about it. Not just for the old man's sake, but because it wouldn't do to do a good deed and not let anyone know about it, would it?

She seldom came over to his little house, except to drop off a basket of food or something from the kitchen wrapped in a clean towel, but he made an effort to keep the place neat anyway. He stopped dropping his dirty work shirts on the floor, and drove nails into the walls so that he could hang them up. He changed the sheets on his bed each week. You never knew . . .

He considered stripping the leaves of the Bible down from his walls, and replacing them with a lick of paint, something blue, maybe, but he balked at the sacrilege. He also wondered what he would read at night if he did that, so he let them be.

On evenings he sat on the porch with his work in his hands, even after it had become too dark to see properly. He stared at the back of her apartment, wondering what was going on inside. He wondered how things were going between Myra and that rebellious daughter she had to deal with. Jacob was convinced that she hadn't been to school in weeks. Every morning the girl left in her school uniform, spic and span, shoes gleaming white, socks turned down just right. And every morning she ducked down one path or another to the river. Didn't teachers call round to a parent's house when a child failed to turn up? They did in his day. Times certainly were changing.

The girl was openly hostile to him. She refused to return his 'Good mornings.' The moment she returned to the house on afternoons, timing herself so that she seemed to be coming back from school, the house seemed to grow hotter and tighter, like all of the air was being sucked out of it. If she came in and caught him there—he used the word 'caught' because she always managed to make him feel guilty—he would find an excuse to leave. No matter what he was doing, he rose to his feet and promised to finish it tomorrow, always giving some reason: he needed a tool that he'd left behind, it was getting too dark, he had to meet a customer, and he'd see Myra tomorrow. And the girl would shoot him a malignant smile that made it clear that she knew why he was leaving. Myra always knew why he was leaving, too, but pretended not to show it. She always nodded vigorously when he explained painfully about this tool that he did not have, and why he'd have to come in to finish the job the next day. Her eyes flicked to the brooding girl who would be watching this exchange with malicious pleasure, but she would nod and say, *Yes, yes, Jacob, no trouble at all. Thank you for coming. Yes, tomorrow morning early would be fine.* Then he would slink gratefully out of the house like a guilty dog.

Odile

Her school skirt was barely pulling closed across her thickening waist, and her breasts felt unnaturally heavy, like they weren't hers. Why the hell did she even bother to go through this damn pretense with the school uniform every morning? The bitch wouldn't care if she went to school or not. All she did was think about that little bastard she was carrying. At night she rubbed cocoa grease into her belly, for the stretch marks, like at her age it was important whether she got marks or not. Odile watched her mother sit at the window and stare out at the tamarind tree and rub and rub her fat belly with her eyes in the distance. The baby was all she thought about. Sometimes Odile caught her whispering softly to it in the dimness. The waves of jealousy made her sick.

Then she kept finding excuses to let in the old man from next door. Odile couldn't come home on an afternoon and he wasn't kneeling down on his twisted leg in the kitchen fixing something or the other, or pretending to fix it. Was Myra blind? He was sniffing around her like a pothound smelling pussy. Never mind it was pregnant pussy. She should be ashamed of herself, smiling and flirting and sending food over for him. She wouldn't give a shit if she found out that Odile wasn't going to school. So what was the point?

Still she got up every morning and bathed, making sure to wrap herself in the thickest towel that she had before she sprinted from the shower to the bedroom to dress. Cover that belly. No sense in letting her see the belly. And she dressed carefully, like a good schoolgirl, with her socks folded over twice and her hair drawn back in one rubber band. *Hold your breath when you pull the skirt closed. Walk with your books in front of you. That's the spirit.* Her mother never noticed. She didn't care.

Rory joined her by the river more and more often. He'd better watch it, she constantly told him. If his father found out, he'd kill him, literally. But Rory didn't seem to care about school or about his father. She found him stranger and stranger these days. Not stranger, more confident. Assertive. She realised that she kept thinking of him as the Rory that used to follow her around with the chicken tucked under his arm, begging her for a game of cricket, the Rory who used to be crestfallen when she cut him dead with some impatient remark, who used to stare at her legs as she passed, pretending he wasn't looking.

Now each time she met him she became more and more aware how fast he was growing. He wasn't shorter than she anymore—in fact he was several inches taller, and easily forty pounds heavier. She stared at him with awe—when did that happen? Seems like she just turned her head for a minute, and there he was, halfway towards being a man.

He was good company anyway. He gave up on the probing questions about her mother and just sat there on the big rock, staring with her into the water. Sometimes he held her hand. Often he brought ripe mangoes for them to share. These they ate hungrily at lunchtime, peeling them with their teeth. When they were done, they threw the skins into the water and watched the fish fight over them.

Odile began to realise that the puppy crush that he had had on her for years was growing into something more power-ful, but never gave it much thought. She wasn't looking for anyone, she scorned the idea of contact with anyone, espe-cially one so young. She hadn't spoken to Blue in more than a month and was sure that he hadn't felt much of a loss. The few moments that she spent mulling over him left her puzzled as to how she could shrug off a relationship that a few months ago she would have died for. She was changing, she supposed. Maybe pregnancy did that to you.

Myra and Odile

Sebastian ate noisily. Myra watched him wearily from across the room. He was getting worse, his eyes were becoming more unfocused, and more often than not he got up in the morning unsure of where he was. Sometimes she heard him tossing in his little bed, muttering. He was feeling the tension in the house and responding the only way he knew how, by distancing himself. She was sure that he was more aware of his surroundings than he gave on, and sure that his withdrawal and disorientation were a means of resistance.

She cut a mango into small bits for him and placed each piece on the small plate. It wouldn't do to let him get his hands on the seed in case he tried to eat it and choked. He hooked each morsel with his claws and slurped it down like a little boy deliberately trying to annoy his mother.

"Slow down, Daddy," she said. Sebastian slurped down another piece. At least none had fallen on the front of his shirt yet. That was a miracle in itself. After a few moments, he got up and walked purposefully out of the kitchen. She supposed he was taking up his post outside the fence. The little pram that had been damaged on that awful day down by the Savannah was beyond repair. She'd spirited its mangled body out of the house one day when Sebastian wasn't looking, and dumped it. He searched for it, sniffling and mewling, for a few days, then seemed to have forgotten about it. He took to walking around with his things in the large wicker basket that she used at the market. He carried it close to his chest and propped it up against the fence when he needed his arms free. She was glad for Jacob's presence; at least she went to work knowing that someone was there to look out for her father. At least she had that much.

She heard Odile moving around in her room. Myra let her breath out in a rush. She longed for the girl to leave the house. She was a bad mother, feeling like that, dying for her child to be anywhere but around her. That made her a bad mother. But she couldn't handle it. She couldn't stand the silences and the glares, the rude responses to the simplest question. What in the name of God had happened to this girl?

She wasn't even going to school anymore. Since the day that Jacob had told her about seeing Odile go down to the river, Myra was convinced that the girl hadn't been to the school more than two or three times. What she could be doing down there she couldn't imagine. It couldn't be a boy: Odile was too young for that, and much too smart. She had her exams next June. She was sulking, that was certain. Myra hoped that at least she opened her books.

What made her feel worse was knowing that she, as Odile's mother, should be doing something about it. She should be calling her on it, saying "I know," and sending her packing to school with a lecture. But she was a coward. Myra admitted to herself that she was terrified of this dark cold child that slept under her roof but did little else. She was glad that the girl had taken to eating her meals in her room. She was glad for the peace at the table, rather than this heavy malignant gloom that seemed to follow Odile around. She was glad the girl avoided her in the corridor and turned abruptly if they met each other in the yard. She didn't want to deal with the whole bloody mess that they were making of their lives. That made her a bad mother, didn't it?

Odile clomped out of her room and past the open doorway. She didn't turn her head towards the kitchen. She didn't look in. Myra watched her as she passed. She was clutching her pile of books before her in the same tiresome daily charade. Good little girl off to school, with all these books. Off to study. Myra held the coffee mug hard with both hands and wished she could pour herself a *real* drink. As soon as the girl left, she promised herself. Just as soon as she's out the door. She could feel it burn in her chest already.

The girl reached out with one hand to open the front door. As she did so, the ludicrous heap of books slipped. The door flew open, and Odile half lunged, half scrambled to catch the precarious pile. They scattered on the floor with the crack of a bullet. She cursed coarsely.

Myra was taken aback by the foreignness of the epithet on her daughter's lips. She leaned forward instinctively as the books hit the floor, then stopped, resisting the impulse to run round and help. As Odile bent forward to gather her belongings, she lost the cover that they had afforded her. She was silhouetted in the bright morning light, and like the caving in of walls, realisation hit her mother.

Myra choked. Her hands flew to her face, and for a bewildering moment she forgot how to breathe. "Odile," she said, finally.

The girl turned. Their eyes met, so alike in clarity and colour that one set could have been the mirror image of the other. Both pairs were wide with horror, pupils dilated, one stunned by the awful discovery, the other by being discovered.

"Odile," Myra said again. The girl didn't even straighten up. What to say, what to say? She set the mug down with infinite care and stood. The books lay clumsily at the girl's feet. Finally she stood up and walked out of the kitchen into the living room and began to gather them up one by one. Biology. Physics. Heavy books. Odile watched as she laid them on the side table. She watched without helping.

"Who did this?" Myra said eventually. The child in her own belly seemed to leap in sympathy with its tiny counterpart, so close was she standing to Odile. "Tell me who it was."

Odile straightened. Her eyes resumed their dark, hateful glare. "Is that all you can say? Who did it?"

Myra searched for words. None came. She opened her mouth to speak, but her wits failed her.

"Is that all?" Odile pressed mercilessly on. "That's all you're interested in? I should have known you'd be thinking of a man first."

"What do you mean?"

"Not 'Odile, how are you?' or 'Odile are you all right?' It's 'Odile, who did you fuck?' Is that all you think of?"

"No . . ."

"I think so."

"No," Myra pleaded with her. "I wasn't thinking. Please."

"Forget it." Angry, she gathered the books to her chest again, though there was no point now. They no longer provided her with a shield from her mother, but still she held them to her chest like armor.

Myra grabbed her by the arm and was shocked to feel how gaunt it was. This girl was an athlete. She was always thick and solid, like Myra herself. But her hand closed around Odile's arm like a bracelet. Shame threw her. The girl had been starving herself, and she hadn't even noticed. Bad mother. "Odile," she said again. "Please, don't go. Talk to me."

"Why?"

"Because we have to."

"Why?" Odile tugged fiercely to free herself.

"Talk to me. I'm your mother."

Odile seemed to find that brutally funny. "*Now* you're my mother? When was the last time you acted like my mother, or anybody's mother other than that thing inside of you that you talk to all the time?"

Myra was stung. Was she really that bad? She prayed for calm; none came. "I talked to *you*, too," she said bluntly.

Odile shot her a withering look. "Not recently," she said. She twisted herself out of Myra's relaxed grip and left the house without looking back.

Rory and Odile

He waited on the rock for her to come. It was another one of those hot days, like all the other hot days before it, when by eight o'clock everywhere else was intolerable except this blessedly cool little part of the river where the bamboo made a whispering roof overhead and cut him off from the spiteful sun. The river had become a refuge for him, a long tunnel which bulged into a darkened private bamboo cave where he could lie on the cool rock and pretend anything he wanted.

Most of the time he was there before Odile, and he clasped those extra minutes close to himself. The rock was a springboard from which he could launch himself into any fantasy. Most of them included Odile. Often he lay on his back with his eyes closed (when your eyes are closed, you can see anything you want to), and Odile would loom over him with her long braids touching his face and those big dark nipples against his chest. She would tell him all sorts of things under her breath. The things she told him made *him* breathe faster, too. All alone in their bamboo cave she told him how strong and handsome he was, and then she slid her tongue like a hummingbird's into his mouth.

Many times when Odile finally joined him at the rock, she found him in a state of agitation, pupils wide and endlessly dark. Usually he was so excited and hard that he was embarrassed and hoped she wouldn't notice, and had to flip over onto his stomach from the time he heard her footsteps down the bank. Even contact with the cold rock on his heated crotch did nothing, and for several minutes after she joined him, he remained lying on his front, as casually as he could, as though nothing in the world was going on.

But even as he tried to contain his conflicting excitement and embarrassment, he knew that Odile was coming round. He could tell by the way she looked at him these days that she was recognising him at last for the man that he had so suddenly become. He wasn't the little neighbour boy anymore. He was a man in his own right, and his pimples were clearing up and Odile was noticing. Soon enough he would lay her down in that rock for real, and furthermore she would want it. She would be asking him for it, begging him, that's what she would be doing. He didn't know when it was going to happen, only that it was going to be soon.

It would be romantic, with the swish of the bamboo overhead, far from the noise of the road and the yard and his father need never find out, and the river would just cruise by and cool their cave. Even the mosquitoes would hold back in reverence when he finally peeled each item of her clothing off her, starting with her school tie and the neat white blouse, then the blue skirt. He already had a place to lay them so they wouldn't be crushed. He'd placed thick bamboo stalks across two stumps, three feet off the ground. That was where they'd lay out their clothes. He was sure she'd want to undress him in turn: that was why every time he came down, he made sure his underwear was decent. He didn't want her to help him take his clothes off and then notice that his drawers had a hole in them or anything.

He lay on his back, letting her phantom kisses fall on his lips and chin and brow until a clumsy thrashing through the bushes on the banks let him know that she had arrived. He didn't have a watch, but he knew that she was later than usual. Automatically he rolled onto his belly, telling himself that soon, when she finally admitted she loved him, he wouldn't have to hide like that. There would be pride rather than embarrassment. He knew she would be impressed by him. As she stripped off her shoes and socks and splashed through the water towards him, he indulged in a twenty-second fantasy wherein he flipped himself over onto his back and gave her a seductive smile, and told her there was a surprise down the front of his pants for her. She undid his pants front eagerly, and when he popped out at her she gasped in delight and awe. It would be the first time she would see a man naked and aroused, and he knew she would be impressed. He ground his hips surreptitiously against the cool, hard stone.

He heard her wade through the water and then haul herself up next to him. As she did so, a book slipped from her grasp and splashed into the water.

"Fuck," Odile said. As it sank, it fanned open, the bright dust cover unfurling like a kite. They watched as it settled on the riverbed. He turned sharply towards her, unused to the sound of obscenities on her lips. Her face was a dark bloom. For a moment he was frightened.

She stared down into the water with her dark face set tight, wondering aloud what it would sound like to the tiny brown fish that huddled close to the rock, wondering whether a 'thud' under water was anything like a 'thud' on land. She threw another book over the side. It settled slowly next to the first. There wasn't any thud that they could discern.

"Maybe you have to be in the water to hear it," she suggested to him. The level sanity of her voice frightened him more than any raving would have. He watched as she threw another and another over the edge. Her notebooks followed, and Rory, now consumed with curiosity in spite of himself, watched her careful notes dissolve into a blue and lavender blur as her education washed itself off the pages. When she was done, she lay back next to him, looking straight up at the bamboo ceiling.

He settled himself down next to her, on his back this time, which the cooling of his body permitted. He tried to follow the direction of her eyes, wanting to share even her silent contemplation by staring at the same patch of bamboo that she was staring at. Neither of them spoke.

Mosquitoes sang high in their ears, irritating sopranos demanding an audience. "Those books were expensive," he said.

"Yeah."

There was another period of silence.

"I hate my mother," Odile said with quiet passion. Rory turned his head. "I hate my mother."

"What did she do?"

"She didn't do, she just is."

"Is what?"

"A fucking bitch. A bitch. That's what she is."

"Why? What did she do?"

Odile threw him a look that made his balls contract. He inhaled sharply, mentally chastising himself. Stupid, stupid, stupid.

"Bitch," Odile repeated with venom. Then her vacant eyes told Rory that her mind was back up in the bamboo ceiling. He waited.

Tears welled up out of the empty eyes and rolled down the sides of her face. He watched as they rolled past the fine dark hairs along her temple and into her ears and he longed to interrupt their flow with his tongue.

The visceral sensuality of the impulse startled him. His limited knowledge of sexual matters had so far confined his fantasies to the most basic rutting, and this single unbidden impulse was for him more erotic than any sweaty carnal fantasy he had ever had. He felt himself growing hard again, and contemplated flipping over to hide his embarrassment. He glanced quickly at Odile, but her spirit was out beyond the bamboo, and the shell that lay next to him on the rock didn't even look at him, much less notice the shameful bulge. He wondered if he would get away with a few furtive caresses to his groin, but abandoned the idea.

The shell that was Odile became reanimated. "I can't go

home," she said. She wiped the tears from her temple, destroying the fine web of his fantasy.

"Why?" He moved closer. His crotch screamed.

She shook her head. "Nothing. I can't. That's all."

"Tell me." He was up on his knees now, pulling her into a sitting position. She did not resist. He faced her with his arms on her shoulders, wanting to shake her until the truth came rattling out of her mouth like teeth. "Why? Tell me!"

Her dull eyes flew to his face and she wavered for a moment. Then she looked at some vague area beyond his shoulder. "No."

He held her arms tighter than he meant to, but instead of shaking her hard until she talked, he was pulling her to him, propelled by the burning in his crotch that had now become a buzzing in his ears. His wet, clumsy kisses fell upon an unresponsive face, but the pure excitement of finally touching her like this was all that he could see or hear or feel. His tongue fought its way into an unresisting mouth and ran along her big hard teeth. Her mouth was a private cave that echoed their cave of bamboo, and Rory explored it excitedly; each tooth was a treasure that he had to stop and touch. He was drowning in his own sweat.

Past cowardice, his hands reached up to the full breasts that lay on a thin cage of ribs. The first encounter with such soft flesh was more than he could ever have created in his make-believe universe. He tugged at her buttons, pulling the blouse up and out of the waist of her school skirt. She made no move to resist. When the blouse was off, he tossed it aside, forgetting the bamboo clothes hanger that he had patiently designed for just this moment.

He placed the flat of his palm against her solid torso; the thickness of it excited him. He'd thought she was skinny, her arms and legs were getting skinny, but under her clothes her middle was solid and fat and the contrast was thrilling.

Her bra confounded him. The hooks defied his trembling fingers until a frustrated cry tore from his chest. Then he felt her hands push his away and deftly unhinge the contraption with the woman's knowledge resident in her fingers.

"Why not?" he heard her say to herself, her very tone a verbal shrug.

It wasn't anything like the passionate declaration of love that she made to him day after day in his dreams, but he was beyond caring about that.

"I won't hurt you," he said, gasping, because that's what men said in the books he'd read. You didn't want them to be scared or anything, especially since it was the first time for them. You had to promise you wouldn't hurt them even when you knew you were really big and that you would.

She didn't resist as he laid her back on the rock and wrestled with his zipper. When he finally pulled himself free, he held it in his hand before her for her inspection, grinning, full of pride. Her eyes flew downwards and then up to his face with an expression that he couldn't read. He guessed it to be fear, and promised again that he wouldn't hurt her, and if he did, the pain wouldn't last long. She smiled when he said it, so he must have convinced her.

With eager hands he tugged her panties down to her ankles. The panties were blue. In his fantasies he was always stumped by what colour they would be. He liked to work out little details like that, and in his fantasies he had tried her with pink and green and white, all sorts of colours, and finally here she was, and she was wearing blue. He brought the bit of material up to his face and inhaled her scent. It was like nothing he had ever smelled before, and he would gladly have drowned in it. He groaned with the feel of thin nylon against his tongue and forgot her lying next to him.

When he looked up, his bright, glowing eyes met her vacant ones, and he set her panties aside on the rock and plunged into her. The dry tissue resisted, but he was in, and she drew her arms around him with a soft gasp of surprise. He crooned in her ear, talk of love rushing off his tongue. Her insides embraced him tighter than he ever thought possible: she would kill him, strangle him, choke off his blood and let him die fighting for his next breath, but death would be sweet. Faster than he expected or imagined, there was pain in his toes and his head and blood before his eyes, and his screams were echoing down the tunnel of the river, carried on the water.

His heart would never return to normal. It beat itself furiously against his ribs like a bird intent on escape, and his throat was constricted, cutting off air. His mind was closed to him, fingers of his spirit reached blindly around inside the darkness of his head to find some thought that he could anchor himself to. Convince himself his mind hadn't shattered. When finally the red curtain before his eyes dissolved, he realised he was still on the rock in the bamboo cave. The realisation came as a surprise.

He looked down at his pliant lover. She lay under him with her eyes closed and her mouth open. He kissed her open mouth and eased himself out of her reluctantly. It was like leaving home. Respectfully, he pulled her skirt back down over her exposed thighs, reluctantly covering the furry triangle even though he ached to bury his face into it and cover it with kisses. The thought alone made him giddy. But he was full of concern for her modesty, and didn't want her to be cold.

"I love you," he said, for the first time in sanity rather than in frenetic ranting.

She looked at him for a long time. "Yes," she nodded.

"And you love me, don't you?" he prompted. Her breasts were exposed, nipples like shiny prunes. No, those he wouldn't cover. He had to allow himself something, after all. He waited for an answer, feeling tension swelling in his mouth like cotton wool.

"Okay," she said. She watched him stare at her breasts without embarrassment.

He stroked her forehead, letting his hands run down her braids. "You all right?"

"Yeah." She sat up and buttoned her blouse. She didn't put her bra back on, so he contented himself with the view of the two dark patches through the thin material.

Rory wondered what you said to a woman after you made love to her. Was there some special protocol? Did convention dictate any particular topics of conversation? He pondered upon this, wondering what Odile was thinking but suddenly too shy to ask. She didn't seem keen on talking anyway.

After a few minutes, he clambered down into the water and retrieved her books. They spread them out on the bank to dry. He withdrew into the bushes to pee and returned with a large white lily. It was topped with tiny pistils that were covered with thick gold dust. If he rubbed it on her cheek and the dust came off, it meant she loved him. He clambered up onto the rock and scattered yellow dust on her unresisting cheek. Then he solemnly handed the blossom to her. She took it with a small smile.

Myra and Odile

With Odile gone, Myra was alone in the house, and the house was full of graves. All around, all the rooms were full of dead things buried just below the surface, just under her feet. With every step, she treaded on something dead, and all the chairs and the tables and the TV and radio were stone monuments without any names on them. The air was thick with flies that tried to get at the corpses underfoot but couldn't get through the dirt so they settled for the dough and fish and meat she'd left out on the kitchen counter.

Myra walked carefully past the big stone that marked the grave of her child and then past the grave of Odile's child to Sebastian's room, which was empty. The bed was empty, although her father's corpse should have been on it. She laid herself out on the narrow bed that smelled of old age, fear, defeat, resignation, and dirt gathering in crevices in ancient skin. With her arms crossed over breasts that were already swelling, she closed her eyes and tried to listen to the dense quietness all around her. She stayed that way while the shadows in the room slowly lengthened, and by the time the sun was on the other side of the house, she was sitting on the edge of the bed with her head in her hands.

This couldn't go on. There was no money. Not for two babies. It would not do Odile to miss school and stay home and mind hers and Myra's instead of getting an education—

which she should have been doing instead of going out getting pregnant by God knows who.

How hadn't she known? Why hadn't she seen? The girl was seventeen, a child, yes, but wasn't she just that age when she'd gone and gotten involved with that fast talker who was to father Odile? Why hadn't she known?

She'd hoped and hoped that no daughter of hers would suffer like she had at the hands of a man. At the prick of a man. She'd promised that she wouldn't let it happen. Yet she kept telling herself that Odile was a good girl, that there was no need for any lectures, not yet. She was young and bright and interested in her schoolwork, so she, Myra, didn't have to sit her down like she wished *her* mother had and warn her about men and their slick, lying tongues and bags of sexual tricks.

So she'd let her daughter down and it was her fault. Too busy in the kitchen kneading dough to see that her daughter was growing up, and to hear her cries for attention and guidance.

What about this baby, no, not a baby yet, this lump of flesh that had a heart and little eyes and fingers but which couldn't think, not yet? Odile couldn't go on. She couldn't have it. Myra wouldn't let her go on and ruin her life and give up her A Levels and maybe university so she could stay at home and wipe up snot and sell smoked herring sandwiches for a living. Myra wouldn't let her.

She'd tell her what to do. There wasn't any choice. She still had the money from Slim in the drawer, and she would make discreet enquiries and find her a good doctor who would use clean tools and give her antibiotics afterwards. And Odile would hate her for it, but a year or two years from now when it was over and when she thought about it less and less, she would understand. When she was benefiting from her education, it would be worth the blood on her mother's hands. Myra would take all the blame, Odile wouldn't have to suffer any guilt, she could always tell herself her mother made her do it. And sleep with a clear conscience.

"My blame," she said to her absent daughter, "not yours."

The rattling in the kitchen startled her for a second until she recognised the shuffling steps of the old man. She rose to her feet—she weighed a thousand pounds—and went quietly to the kitchen entrance and watched him as he rooted around for food. Just to make sure he didn't try to cut anything with a sharp knife or eat butter or lard on its own. Sebastian found a packet of biscuits and turned, shuffling slowly past her as though she were a ghost. He walked out into the yard and out the front gate. Through the vine-covered fence she could see him squatting on the pavement at the side of the road, sharing his lunch with the ants.

If only he could pass away quietly in his sleep, she thought, ashamed that the idea that lurked in her heart at a barely discernible level could have the temerity to rise to the level of consciousness. Nothing painful, no awareness of death, just a quiet slipping through the doorway, from one state to the other. He would be far from the reaches of pain then. Back with his wife, if that sort of thing really happened.

Was that the solution, to kill her problems, let them die so that she wouldn't have to think about them or face them or endure the weight of her own guilt? She begged God's forgiveness: she didn't mean it, she didn't wish her father dead, forget she ever thought anything, lest she wake up in the morning to find her wish granted during the night and no one but herself to blame, and the death certificate reading 'death by wishing.'

When the house began to darken, she was amazed that the day had slipped so swiftly into night and she had barely moved a muscle. She cleared up the spoilt food on the counter and tossed lumps of uncooked dough into the garbage, chiding herself on another day wasted. It was becoming a habit now, and soon enough her customers would realize that she was no longer reliable, and wander off to find another place to eat. She didn't need to lose that income now.

Odile came in after seven, disheveled with mud on her school shoes, no pretense now of having gone to school. She walked past her mother and into her room, slamming the door. But Myra was too fast for her, and as the door swung shut, she slid her arm in, receiving a painful bruise that she never noticed.

The girl squared her shoulders, prepared for battle, hostile as only a teenager could be. Her mother stood by the closed door, angry welt rising on her uncaring arm, searching for a place to start.

"I'm sorry," Myra said at last.

Odile had been expecting an assault. She was floored. "What for?" she asked gruffly. From the set of her brow and jaw, she wasn't prepared to give an inch.

"I don't know." Myra lifted her shoulders and let them drop. "I should have looked after you."

The girl rolled eloquent eyes into her head. "Oh, please!"

"I should have done something."

"You didn't." The black, venomous eyes were now fixed on her face like darts.

Myra nodded. "I didn't know, I mean . . . I had no idea."

"No idea what? That I was screwing?"

Myra winced at the image but nodded.

"You think I'm a child. I'm always a child for you. Well, I'm not."

Yes you are, Myra thought but did not say.

"I'm not a child and haven't been for a *long* time. And don't think it was just one. It wasn't just one man. It was lots. Okay?"

There had been a time when Myra, too, judged her own maturity by the number of men she'd slept with. It hurt her to see another woman, more so her daughter, buy into the same old lie. "That don't make you a woman." She wanted her daughter to know that.

"It don't make me a child." The girl was more sullen and childlike than ever.

Myra didn't dispute this. There was much more at stake. "Odile," she began, "do you want it?"

Her eyes grew round. "What?"

"I'm asking you if you want it. The baby. Do you want it?"

"What do you mean? I *got* it."

"Yes, girl. But do you *want* it. To have it."

The girl watched her suspiciously. "No choice."

"There is a choice."

"What do you mean?" She was genuinely bewildered at first, until knowledge and realisation flooded her face.

Myra waited.

"No."

"It's the only way."

"No."

"You have to think of school."

"I can't."

"Please. I have money." Mention of the money brought the memory of another such argument galloping through Myra's skull. Weeks ago, she'd stood in this same house, having this same discussion with Slim, only she got to be the good guy and wear the halo and declaim the sanctity of life. Shame and self-loathing rose in her throat and made her mouth bitter.

"No, Ma!" the girl pleaded, hands up over her face. "I can't. Don't make me!"

I wish I could make you, Myra thought, *I wish I could drag you off kicking and screaming, and in a few hours it would be all over and you'd hate me but I'd have given you your life back.* But she folded her hands across her own slight bulge, as though protecting it from having to listen to all this talk of murder, and said softly, "I can't make you, child. Just think about it. At least think."

Odile turned to the window and stared out into the darkness. Myra waited five minutes, then ten, for a word from her daughter, and none was forthcoming. Silently, she withdrew from the room.

Jacob and Myra

She'd aged a dozen years since he last saw her—when? The day before? Two days? Her skin was without the glow that always made him stare, and her eyes were rimmed with darkness. Her regal cheekbones—Jacob liked to think of them as her Queen of Sheba cheekbones—came close to piercing her skin.

He let her into his small room and listened without interrupting as she gasped breathlessly on about Odile being pregnant, how the child kept insisting she wasn't a child, about Sebastian dying in her heart. She and her daughter both pregnant? Could that happen? He thought of the thin, hostile child: she looked deathly ill, surely that pregnancy could not be normal. She was growing thinner and more drawn every day.

"Are you sure," he said at last. "Are you sure she's pregnant?"

"Sure," Myra sobbed. "She's sure."

"Not sick?"

"Maybe both," Myra said. "I don't know."

"She's so thin," he mused.

"Yes."

"What are we going to do?" He heard himself say that 'we,' and to him it sounded right. There was a 'we,' wasn't there? He looked at her quickly to see if she'd noticed, but she sat across from him in the denseness of his stuffy living room cradling her head. He wondered if he should get up and turn on another light or make some coffee or something, make himself useful.

"I don't know," Myra answered. "Really. I don't know."

"Tomorrow you'll be able to think," he said. He reached across the small space between them and stroked her brow, which was hot and bright as though she were consumed by a fever.

"Did you eat?" She looked so tired.

"I don't know."

"Eat, then," he said. He got painfully to his feet and moved towards the little kitchen.

She raised a hand to stop him. "No, Jacob. I'm not hungry."

"You have to." He hesitated in the doorway.

"I'd be sick."

"Then drink something."

She nodded. "Yes. Strong."

He made two cups of strong, bitter coffee, embittered all the more by a generous amount of brandy, and brought them to where they were sitting. She drank hers as though it were not boiling hot. He watched her as she drained the last of her cup before his was cool enough to drink. She set the cup on the floor and sat back in the chair with her face tilted to the ceiling and her eyes closed. He sipped his drink thoughtfully.

She was unmoving for so long that he thought she might have fallen asleep. When she finally moved, he was taken by surprise. "Sit with me," she said, holding out her arms.

He rose and came to stand before her.

"Sit," she insisted, tugging at his hands until he knelt at her feet, ignoring his screaming hip. She put her hands on his shoulders and brought his head to her lap. Through the cotton skirt he could smell her. Her scent rose like vines, like fingers in those cartoons where you got hooked by the nose and pulled closer and closer. The warmth of her reminded him of a stone wall in the late-afternoon sun, giving off heat as you passed by. He put his head down in her lap, comforted by the warmth and the scent but guilty because she was the one in need of comfort, not he.

He felt her hands on his shoulders and on the back of his neck. His broad, hard shoulders made him feel clumsy, like a bull. But she ran her hands down them in rhythmic appreciation, nails scraping the coarse material of his shirt, and he relaxed, content to squat here forever and inhale this wonderful smell.

He looked up and there were fresh tears on her cheeks, and he knew that this time the tears were for herself, not for her daughter. She was on her knees beside him and her eyes were closed, face upturned, waiting to be kissed, but he couldn't. She was upset and in trouble and had had a bellyful of brandy, and if he did, he knew where it would lead. And then the next day when her tears had dried and the brandy was gone, she'd look at him with horror and ask herself how, *how* could she have let it happen?

"Please," she whispered. The smells of coffee and brandy battled on her warm breath.

He tasted the coffee, and the brandy, and wild fruit that didn't grow anywhere on the planet. Her warm mouth engulfed him in desperation and need, and he tried to give her as much as he could, in spite of his own hunger. He tried to pour comfort and consolation and strength and reassurance down into her with his mouth. Their kisses were seasoned with salt from her eyes.

They struggled to their feet; she laughed softly at his clumsiness, but not unkindly so, and even though he regretted being unable to make any grand gesture such as sweeping her into his arms and whisking her to the bed, they found their way to it all the same. It was covered with old clothes and books and she tossed them to the floor, dusting it off with a pillow. He wished he'd kept a neater house. He wished he'd shaved.

How they fit on the single bed, he didn't know. It groaned under them; he hadn't bought it with a woman in mind. She smiled when it squeaked, so he forgot about feeling badly about its size and its construction.

"Kiss me again," she insisted. He complied. He felt her eager hands tugging at the buttons on his shirt, so he made matters easier by pulling it up over his head. She followed suit, not waiting for him to undress her, tugging off her dress and bra and panties until she was naked long before he was. He looked down at her in the dim light of the single bulb and gasped. Her skin was as smooth as a seal's.

Clumsily he got up and found the lamp and flicked it on. "I want to leave it on," he told her. "I have to look at you."

She nodded and waited expectantly, greedy eyes upon him. He removed his pants almost apologetically, revealing the grotesque, distorted scar that ran from his hip to his knee. As he stood at the bed, listing to one side, she got to her knees and examined him with the unembarrassed curiosity of a small child. The wheals and red flesh were like coarse bits of rope running off in different directions. She let her fingers trail each meandering scar. He stood, subjecting himself to her examination with embarrassment, yet more excited than he ever remembered himself being.

When she turned her attention away from his twisted leg and took him in her mouth he was completely taken aback. He gasped and almost fell forward onto her, throwing his arms up and out to the walls for support. He wanted to let the pleasure overwhelm him, ride the wave to the end, but he wanted even more to sink into her, squelch into her until they got so close that nobody could tell them apart. He withdrew gently and climbed into bed next to her, shushing her anxious questions, that no, nothing's wrong, yes, it was fine, only . . .

"Only I like it better this way, face-to-face with you." The light of the lamp was bright, and he indulged himself, looking her over, down the sharp bones of her throat to the full breasts and to the bulge of her abdomen. "Will it be all right?" he asked, cupping the bulge. "With this, I mean."

"Oh, yes," she assured him. She tugged at him eagerly.

Hungry but curious, he delayed even further, letting his hands drift downwards past the wonderful hump of her belly and over her broad hips until his hands encountered soft, curly hair. He parted her lips lightly, thinking of flower petals.

"Please," she insisted, and he abandoned all attempts to draw out the moment. He lowered himself into her and she reached up to meet him halfway. He marveled at how well they fit together, and that was his last conscious thought. All he could do next was feel. Her arms and legs were wrapped around him. Even his hip ceased its complaints. He felt her lips in the matted hair on his chest, on his throat, felt her nails scratch him, and felt her clenching him in her hungry grasp.

One of them was crying. He shuddered in disbelief, and for a second or two remembered all those women in Grande and Town and Toco and San Fernando and Point and wondered how come none of them ever made him feel like this.

The brightness of the light made the room even hotter, and they lay close together with her beautiful long legs twisted around his ugly, scarred ones, and fought to regain their breath.

"Behold, you are fair, my love," he whispered when the room was still again. "Behold, you are fair. You have a dove's eyes."

"What?" She squinted at him.

He was delirious, laughing out loud. "It's on the wall over your head. Song of Solomon."

She nodded. "Oh." She'd never read it.

"Eyes like a dove," he repeated. He could smell the sweat that rose in waves from her hair. The rise and fall of his chest slowed as he dozed on her shoulder.

Odile

Too much. It was more than she could handle, all this. Her mother saying please eat, you have to eat in your condition, even though Odile knew in her heart of hearts that her mother wished the thing dead. Even she herself refusing to eat because the idea of food made her sick. She never wanted to eat again, not while the creature floated around inside her in a bag of murky water with its lidless black eyes fixed upwards, blob of a head thrown back, mouth wide open waiting for food to come pouring down her gullet. Eyes like a crayfish, dark and unseeing, like those of any creature that never saw light. Pink veins and transparent skin, tail tucked around itself like a contented salamander. It nauseated her to think that she was forced to carry it around, through no choice of hers, and couldn't shake it loose.

Yet what her mother was suggesting was madness. Her soul was outraged at the suggestion. At night she squirmed in bed, seeing herself damned to hell for the slaughter, looking up out of the burning lake and seeing the half-formed round face peering back down at her from the clouds. It would go to heaven where she never could, automatically, without even having to stand judgment. Like moving up to a higher class at school without taking an exam. She would spend eternity looking up at it, with it looking down at her and wondering what it would have been like to be alive, just for a moment.

Each morning her bed was soaked with sweat, and she had to put fresh sheets on.

Myra never repeated her suggestion, but it was implied in every glance. Odile sensed her mother waiting. And waiting.

She didn't see Rory the next day, nor the next. She knew he was down at the river, but there was no need for pretense, no need to dress up in her uniform and set off as though for school. She was content to sit in her room and simply let the time pass. Day always turned into night, which always turned into day. The predictability was comforting.

She felt no embarrassment at what had passed between them the last time they were together, but felt no particular interest or warmth, either. She'd let him do as he pleased, that was all. She knew that for him it was a moment of novelty and excitement, and that was fine. But as for her, while she'd felt him with her body and knew he was there and knew what he was doing to her, her mind had hovered above them, looking down at the two of them on the rock with scant interest before swooping off to a place she'd created for herself where she could be alone. Rory had taught her that.

The third night he knocked on her wall as he had done before. She rose and went to the window to meet him.

"Odile." He said it like a magic word.

She sat in the window looking down at him. The moon was hazy tonight, surrounded by a halo that broke up into colourful rings of light.

"Odile," he said again. He reached a hand up to her. She hesitated and allowed him to take hers. He stood on the tips of his toes at the high window to bring her hand to his face. She felt the soft beginnings of a beard with shock. She hadn't noticed that before.

"Come down," he begged. She thought about it for a moment and shrugged inwardly. She threw her legs down the side and jumped without warning, confident that he would catch her. He gathered her into his arms. Her feet did not touch the ground.

"You going to put me down?" she asked. The question

was wasted. His beefy arms encircled her hips as he held her above him. His face pressed against her ribs between her breasts. She expected a surreptitious squeeze or bite, some caress, a straying hand down the roundness of her buttocks, but he just stood there without moving, with her looking down on the top of his head. He held her without effort; she was a privilege to hold, not a burden.

When at last he set her down, he put his finger on her lips, silencing her before she even opened her mouth. She followed him round to the front to the tamarind tree. The tree leaned in towards the house, creaking in the high night wind. It sounded like the bones of an old man. Odile sat on the hard-packed earth next to Rory, never mind the cold earth against her bottom, chilling her flesh through her scant underwear. With one accord they looked up at the dark-gray clouds scudding across the face of the moon. These clouds were dense, of substance, evoking not cotton-wool puffs but smooth, beaten lead.

"Rain." Odile sniffed the air.

"Not rain," he contradicted her. "Not possible. It hasn't rained in months. I think it's forgotten how."

"It *is* rain," she insisted. "Smell the air. Smell the dirt. Smell the tree. It's rain. It's got to be."

He sniffed loudly. His broad nostrils flared wide as he greedily inhaled, sniffing everything up and keeping it to himself. "Rain," he finally agreed.

"When, you think?"

He closed his eyes and turned his face to the leaden sky, lips pursed, kissing the wind. "Soon. It's coming down from the hills. You can hear the trees and the grass waiting. It's like they know."

"They do know. They're all awake and watching the sky, just like us. When it's here, they're going to come alive again. They'll get to grow instead of lean forward in the dirt and hide from the sun. They must be so excited, all the plants." She hoped he didn't find her ridiculous, babbling about the plants.

He nodded and leaned into her with his arm around her shoulder. They looked up at the sky again. The clouds chased each other around like horses. Odile waited for him to do something, try to kiss her, slide his hand down past her shoulders to her breasts, like any boy would do. That's what it was all about, sly games. Wait till they're not looking. Slide your hand down. Get a feel, make a pass, steal a kiss.

He did nothing. She could see the scudding clouds reflected in his eyes. She'd been steeling herself for him to say something, anything, about the morning down by the river. But he sat like a man who was simply content to be close to her. There was no crowing, no bleating, no familiar need to prise from her confessions of how great he was, how good it had been. He was just content to be there. The feeling was new to her. She sat quietly and savored it.

The first drops surprised her with their sharpness and intensity. They stung like rubber bullets. They fell on her face and arms and legs, fell on the tree and hit the roof with loud *pings*. A rustling whisper arose in the mountains behind them, whooshing down the slopes, passing from blade to blade of grass like the old game of Chinese telephone, growing more and more intense with each repetition. It shushed through the branches of the tree above them and was taken up by the dry leaves and wilting grass around them. The valley took up the cry, with the frogs and crickets and cicada joining like a choir at practise. The valley hummed.

It's beautiful, Odile thought. A shiver of excitement ran through her. Her skin pulled taut.

The sharp blades of rain tore at their skin and hair until she and Rory raced each other for the cover of the eaves. The hail of bullets became a deluge, and they stood under the eaves smelling the rain and the mud it was making and thinking of how their river must be leaping and dancing out there in the dark without anyone there to see it.

"Rain!" Rory whispered. He couldn't believe it. The moon's halo whirled around it like a shiny spinning hoop.

Odile felt the laughter surge up and out of her before she

could stop it. She didn't recognise the voice with its streak of the old her in it. She'd thought that Odile was dead, but here she was using her tired mouth to laugh out of. She'd only been hiding. She felt Rory's eyes on her face and saw his raw pleasure at her own pleasure and realised that no one had ever been so unselfishly happy for her before. It made her laugh all the more.

The weary old galvanized roofing had forgotten what it was like to feel the rain. It groaned in surprise, a crotchety old man roused from dreaming of his younger days. It split, cracked. Their shelter became useless as slashing rain came in sideways. Rain battered them and doubled its assault by finding its way through ancient nail holes in the eaves.

He took her hand and tugged her hard. She followed without complaint. Round the back, at her window, she was up in his arms, high above his head, being stuffed hurriedly through the window, screaming with laughter, wanting to play now. They'd waited so long for rain, and here he was anxious for her, stuffing her through the window, shouting that he didn't want her to catch cold, it was late, *don't fight me, Odile.* She resisted, grabbing on to the windowsill. He prised her fingers loose and heaved her in. She hit the floor with a thump that she was sure would wake up her mother, but the roar of the rain seemed to wrap itself round her gleeful laughter and cloak the whole house.

When she was finally in, he let himself laugh, too. He stood under the window barefoot in what was rapidly becoming mud and let the water run down his nose and into his mouth. His teeth gleamed. "Dry yourself off," he commanded.

She stood at the window. She was laughing too much to listen.

He leaped at the window and was hanging there by both hands, clinging like a lizard. "Dry off and get into bed"—he threw a threatening leg over the windowsill—"or I'll do it for you."

"No, no," she pleaded. Her stomach hurt with laughter. He looked like he meant it. She wondered what her mother would say if she were to come in at this time of night and see him there, hanging like a monkey, laughing like an insane thing. She swatted at him. "Go away now. Go on. Go home."

"Dry yourself off," he warned her again. He dropped to the ground and was gone.

When she had dried herself off and crawled back into bed, she fancied she could feel him on the other side of the wall, stretched out alongside her. The warmth of his body permeated the wall until she could feel the exact spot where he was lying. She moved closer to the wall and pressed into it. "Just for tonight," she murmured to herself. It was a new experience for her, being loved. Above the roar of the rain she was sure she could hear him breathe.

Sebastian

His wife was sitting at the foot of his bed. She looked good. She was wearing that dress he liked so much with the little yellow flowers, and she didn't have her lovely thick hair tied up in a net like she always wore it. It was combed out dark and fluffy around her shoulders, and it smelled like jasmine.

She was telling him some joke. Although he couldn't see her lips move, he got the joke and laughed out loud at it. *Funny one*, he told her. *Tell me again.* She told him again and he laughed again, more loudly this time.

She tilted her head back and sniffed the air. She closed her eyes with pleasure like she did when he kissed her. "Rain, Sebastian," she told him.

He looked at her sitting at the foot of his bed in the moonlight. He had a wide grin on his face, like it was another of her jokes.

"No," she insisted. She creased her brow to convey her earnestness. "Rain."

He turned to the window. For the first time, the smell hit him. It was like a wave crashing down from the mountains, that smell. Bigger than the mountain. It rumbled like thunder and invaded his nostrils and made his bones ache. He closed his eyes and inhaled.

When he opened his eyes she'd left, just like that, but he was used to her coming and going. Sebastian got up off the bed and shuffled down the corridor to Myra's room. He tapped tentatively on the door. When she didn't answer, he turned the doorknob and went in. He must wake the child up. Her mother would want her to see this.

She gasped and sat ramrod straight in the bed, fear in her eyes. "Daddy?" she cried. Her eyes were like fried eggs.

"Rain," he said simply. He pointed at the window.

She stood next to him and patted his hand. "No, Daddy," the girl said. "It isn't raining."

"Yes," he insisted. "Rain. Your mother says."

Her eyes grew wider yet and her mouth made an O, but then the sound of the rain swept down on the house like rice falling on a tin tabletop.

"Yes," Sebastian said.

Now her eyes turned to joy and she ran to the window. He stood at the window, too, and together they looked up. The moon was wearing a wedding veil of all colours.

"Yes," he insisted. "Rain."

His little daughter put her arms around him and they looked up at the sky. "It *is* raining," she said. She was smiling like a banana.

"I just said that," he chided her. He felt her arms around his chest. The sky turned white with water.

Jacob

He lay on his back in the dark listening to the sound of the rain on the roof. The rain kept the heat in: it was like someone had overturned a huge metal bowl over the little house, not letting any air in, and was dribbling hard little peas out of their hand onto the bottom of the bowl. The peas pinged on his roof and rolled down the slanted sides to the ground.

He tried to picture Myra in her own house in her own room lying on her bed listening to the rain. Myra in her bed with the covers tossed off because of the warm, moist air that was rising up all around them like steam as the rain hit the thirsty dirt outside. On her back, with the covers down at the bottom of the bed, tossed off because of the cloying heat. He sensed her, felt her mind probe outwards searching for his, and wondered why her need was not great enough to cause her to cross the space between them, in spite of the rain.

Her image blurred behind his eyes, because for some reason he couldn't fix it. There were so many little details he didn't know: was she in her underwear, naked, in a nightgown? Would the nightgown be cotton or nylon? He wished he knew. Jacob was not an imaginative man; his mind refused to fill in the blanks for him. So he contented himself with the image of her lying in bed listening to the rain at the same time as he, only around her midsection the image was fuzzed for lack of information.

Funny he didn't know even such a simple thing about a woman with whom he'd shared so much just days ago. He knew how the nape of her neck got damp when she made love. He knew the shape and feel of her dark nipples. He knew her navel was deep enough to accommodate the first joint of his index finger. He didn't know what she wore to bed.

Confounded by ignorance, he let the image fade as he became flooded with questions that needed to be answered. What were the sheets like on her bed? Did she sleep on her back or her front? Did she snore? Fantasy was no good when you had to interrupt it to deal with the practicalities of the thing.

The peas falling on the roof intensified until they became a deafening cascade of tiny metal balls, pounding the roof, the windows, the doors. He listened to the galvanized roofing sigh. It was his first heavy rain in the little house. He listened to the new sounds with the curiosity of a schoolboy. The wind came from the porch side. Tomorrow his workbench would be drenched. He'd never thought of bringing any of his things inside at night. Tomorrow the leather would stink of tannin. Water left stains in leather. He should have thought of that.

His mind made a swooping circle and came back to Myra.

Myra and Odile

When she was a small child, five or thereabouts, she couldn't exactly remember, her father gave her a toy that he had picked up for her the only time he'd gone to America. It was a box that was painted white, with stars of yellow and blue and red along the sides. The box had an arm of some sort poking out the side that you could crank and crank, and the box played music. It played 'Pop Goes the Weasel.' She used to sing along. Then without any warning at all, while she was winding up the arm and singing happily along, the lid of the box snapped open and a big laughing clown popped right out at her.

The first time the clown popped out she was terrified. She ran around in circles, howling, ran for her mother, wondering how her father could have done this to her, given her such a pretty music box with a monster inside. Her mother soothed her and stroked her hair and picked up the box and pushed the clown back down inside it. Then she wound it back up again, singing along in the bright, clear voice that she had. This time when the clown popped out, Myra laughed the fine, high laugh of a child who was still a little scared but who was sure that having her mother around would make everything right. Her mother handed the box back to her and went about her business.

Myra kept playing with the box, partly out of a stubborn desire to overcome her fear of the leaping clown and partly out of the jolt of pleasure she received at surprising herself. It was tempting fate, and mastering that fate—by being able to force the thing back into the box when she wanted—had made her feel confident and strong.

The rain outside was getting on her nerves. It had rained all the first night, throughout the second day, and was now well into the second night. It pounded rhythmically and insistently on the roof, thrumming in the air.

Confined to the house, the three of them were restless, but kept to their rooms. Myra passed her daughter's room with a sense of unease. She could feel the pressure building up in there and inside her daughter. The walls of the room seemed to be slowly swelling, filling up with the girl's unhappiness and resentment and fear until Myra was afraid that it would all expand until it exploded with a deafening blast. Myra was afraid that when it did, she would be right in the path of the flying debris.

She paced restlessly, up the corridor and back. The flooring was already absorbing the moisture of the air and was sticky to her bare feet. She went in search of her slippers, grateful for the little errand that would provide her with at least a minute or two of distraction.

Feet shod, she returned to hover before her daughter's door. It was late, but she sensed—knew—that Odile was not asleep. She could hear the whirring of the troubled mind on the other side. The old spring bed creaked softly as the girl shifted uncomfortably, but in spite of the drumming of the rain and the door between them, the sound tugged against her nerves like a faulty violin bow.

"Odile," she said softly, and tapped on the door. It was a new thing, tapping on Odile's door. Before, when she still kept her daughter locked away in the time-frozen part of her mind that saw her only as a small child, she had come and gone in the girl's room with the same ease with which she accessed any other part of the house. Now she admitted to herself that the girl was entitled to her own little piece of space, not just within the house that they shared but in her mind and in her life. So Myra stood tentatively at the door and knocked.

After a time, the door swung open and the young woman stood there in a long T-shirt. Her eyes were rimmed with exhaustion.

"Can I come in?" Myra asked. The words were strange on her tongue.

Odile's tired eyes widened. She swayed for a moment before standing aside to let her in. Myra didn't bother to flick on the light. They stood facing each other in the grayness of the night with the path of light let in by the open door giving them just enough illumination to see by.

Myra looked around the room as for the first time. She looked at the pictures on the wall and the cluttered writing desk and the clothes on the floor, and wondered about the person who owned all of this. She wondered how much there was about this person that she'd never taken the time to find out.

"I'm worried," she began. She tried not to ask herself what she would say next.

Odile grunted, not encouraging, but not turning her away.

"Are you okay? You're so thin."

Odile shrugged.

"Odile." She took a step closer and put her hand on her daughter's upper arm, encountering papery skin and a length of bone that was all too close to it. "Please eat. Come out and let me cook for you. I'll cook anything you like. Just eat something, please."

"What," she replied. "You mean there aren't any leftovers?"

"Leftovers?"

"Leftovers. Whatever you couldn't sell. Whatever you didn't give away to everybody."

Her blood accelerated in her veins. There was a popping in her ears.

Odile went on. "What are you going to do? Make me fresh soup and feed it to me, make yourself feel better after all those years of left-over food and left-over attention and left-over time, after you're finished giving to everyone else? You going to hand-feed me like you hand-feed Gramps and clean up my messes and look at me for a change instead of giving me five minutes or ten minutes of your time to ask me how was my day and if I've done my homework and not wait for an answer?"

Myra watched the face with the wild, sunken eyes and realised how much Odile had grown to look like her. It was like looking at her own angry face in the mirror. She hadn't realised they were now the same height.

"I did the best I could," she said. She tried to keep her voice level, and to still the mounting pressure in her chest. "I work hard, Odile."

"Yeah."

"It's hard work. You know how early I have to get up. And how difficult it is to make ends meet. And your grandfather takes up a lot of my time. I'm doing the best that I can."

"Well, you didn't do good enough. You don't even see me. You brought that Slim in the house, and you know I hate him. You brought him here and in your bed and you didn't care that I could hear you. You think that's anything for me to hear? You and that noise and that nasty yellow man in your bed, like you have no shame. At least I did my business in *private*."

Myra winced.

"I bet you don't know he used to say things to me," Odile went on. "I bet you never even looked up and saw him looking at me. You thought Slim was so wonderful. You don't know he'd have fucked me if I'd let him. You didn't know because you never looked."

A strange dread rose up in her. "Did he touch you?"

She snorted. "No, but you wouldn't have noticed if he had. You never thought I was worth noticing. You treated me like a little girl. That's what makes it so bad. You never thought he would even *look*. You didn't notice I was pregnant until

I was five months gone. Anybody else would have seen it earlier. They'd have seen it in school, if I'd gone. But not you. You didn't notice because you never thought it was possible. You didn't think it would happen because you still think I'm a little girl. You're still buying me ribbons for my *hair*." Her thin chest heaved with the hurt of years.

Myra stood silent for a long time. What could she say? Motherhood had taken her by surprise, and she'd thought she was doing a good job, but it seemed that she wasn't after all. And now the process was about to repeat itself, this motherhood minefield, twice over. She fixed her eyes on Odile's slightly bulging belly. Odile followed the direction of her gaze and put her hand up to it in an instinctive protective gesture.

"And now you want me to get rid of this so the whole world won't see your mistakes. You should have prevented it before it started. Don't try to cover it up now."

Myra rose to her own defense. "That's not true. I'm not covering anything up. I'm not ashamed of you. I'm concerned for you. I'm worried about your future. And it's not fair to blame me for your pregnancy. You could have done something about that. I can't be with you every minute of the day. And you're a bright girl. You have access to information that I never had. So don't blame me. You could have protected yourself. You were careless, not me."

"Oh, so you're *concerned*," she sneered.

"Yes, I'm concerned."

"Why?" Her eyes held a challenge that Myra barely had the courage to take up.

"Because I don't want you to lose your life. All your opportunities. I don't want the baby to take your life away from you."

"Like I did to you?"

Myra winced. "No," she began to explain, but the explanation was a tangled nettle in her mouth. "You didn't take my life away. It was hard . . ."

"I was a burden. You can say it, you know." Her daughter

goaded her, as if she needed to hear the words of rejection fall from her mother's lips.

"No, you weren't a burden." Myra held her hands up to ward off the venomous attack. "You weren't a burden. It was hard, but I loved you. I did everything I could for us to be okay."

"So I wasn't a burden for you, but my baby will be for me? What you think that makes you? A superwoman?"

"No, no, no," Myra protested. "Why don't you just listen to me? Why don't you let me talk?"

"Talk, then." The girl folded her arms across her chest and stood scowling, just inches from her face.

"I loved you and I wanted you to be happy, but I don't want you to go through what I did. I don't want you to be stuck where I'm stuck."

"Where I put you," Odile said.

Myra couldn't respond. She couldn't deny the unavoidable truth, but to affirm it would sting like a slap. "I just want you to be happy," she said finally. "That's all. I want things to be the way they were before. I want to give you your life back, and your education, and all your dreams."

"And it doesn't matter to you that a part of me will die?"

Myra realised that her very voice was trembling. "Yes, Odile, it matters. But it matters more to me that the rest of you will live."

"How would you feel," Odile said, "how would you feel if someone had done this to you? How would you feel if someone had asked you to do this?"

Myra bit her lip. "I don't know," she lied at last. She felt defeated. She felt Odile's hurt and disappointment all round her. She took a deep breath. "Can I cook you something to eat?"

Odile shook her head and looked pointedly at the door. Myra left.

In her own room, in the damp, wide bed, she longed for Jacob. She wished she could run out through the gray rain, through the mud in the backyard over to his house. There she could feel the strength of his dense arms around her and the bristly hair of his chest against her face, and know that he would listen to her without passing judgment. She'd ask him to tell her another story about the stickfights in the forests of Grande, then ask for another and another until she fell asleep in his arms. She wanted to wake up to find herself in bed with a man who wouldn't pull his clothes on and run away. Who'd greet the morning by immersing himself in her body and surrounding her with his smell.

The desire to leave and run into the night, across the yard, was torturous, but the condemnation of her daughter forced her to stay where she was. When at last she fell asleep, she dreamed of music boxes with arms that churned round and round.

Rory

The damp closed in on him like a clammy blanket. It hung in the air and surrounded the house and touched his face and the bed and the walls and the floor. The air inside his head, in the space behind his nose, expanded, putting pressure on his skull and giving him a throbbing headache that was now two days old.

When he realised that the rain wasn't stopping, he'd tried to let Gracie in. She was soaked through, and her feathers were limp and sad. His father discovered her and tossed her out into the sheeting rain, threatening chicken soup if the rain got any worse. Rory sat by the window looking out at her on the porch. She sat sorrowfully in the furthest corner, damp and bewildered. He thought again of the day when he would get up and walk right out of his father's house and never look back. Get up, take his clothes and his chicken, and go out somewhere and be a man. That day was coming.

He liked to fantasise about the moment. It would be one of great confrontation, a battle between men, when his father would finally realize that he was a man in his own right and didn't have to settle for his grudging handouts. Didn't need to take his father's shit and old talk and threats and blows. In fact, he hoped it *would* come to blows. Hoped for a big showdown between him and the old man. After all these years of silent resistance, he would come out from his other place, his private universe, with no need to hide anymore, and meet his father on his own terms. It was going to be good.

Confined to the small space, the two men avoided each other. Rory passed much of the time thinking of Odile and the night out under the tree when the rain had come, and of the day down at the river. He lay for hours in bed with her somewhere on the other side, and revisited every sensation. He remembered the sharpness of the rock under his knees. The mosquitoes biting, and him not giving a damn.

It was dizzying, the thought of what she had given him on that rock. Showed him a doorway out of that other place where he was spending too much time lately. Let him feel flesh with his hands and his lips rather than with his mind. Fantasy became reality so seamlessly that it still seemed to go on and on somewhere in his head, a never-ending scene, making love on a loop.

He wished the rain over and done with now. When it was over and the sun was out again, he'd take her down to the river where he would feel the agonising pain of sinking into her again and feel the bright humming of blood in his ears. The promise of it brought an ache to his groin that his own touch could not still.

Myra and Jacob

"I waited for you last night," he said. "I heard your mind over the sound of the rain. I felt you wanting to be here."

His boldness surprised her. His acuity did even more. "I did. I thought of you. How did you know?"

"I can hear you turn in your bed. I can hear you sigh in your sleep. Didn't you know that?" He was smiling.

She stood just in the doorway watching him smile at her, seeing a new courage in him, a squareness to the shoulders that hadn't been there before. He stood aside to let her pass, pulled the door quickly behind her, shutting out the white wildness outside. He pulled her by the hand across the small room to the bed. It had clean sheets on it.

She watched him as he walked: his stride was just a little longer. It seemed to her that where he walked before like a wounded soldier, he walked now with the stride of a man who had a new fire in him. With a deep feminine knowledge she recognised the source of that fire to be herself. The idea of it thrilled her. Where there was a bitter sullenness, there was now a glimmer of the man he had been before. She saw now the gleam of the master stickfighter in his eye.

She'd done it. That was the most awesome thing. It was *her* arms and *her* breasts and *her* pussy that he'd touched and grounded himself by. She felt like a creator, some small goddess who could wave her hand and speak to death, and death would listen and stand in abeyance.

She refused to lie next to him. She wanted to stand back for a while, allow the moment to stay just out of her grasp for a short time, before she seized it. When he saw that she wasn't coming, he undressed himself quickly and lay back with his head propped against the wall, letting her look. She looked.

He was huge, stretched out on the bed naked, filling her eyes and her senses. His skin was as black as any she had ever seen, incredibly smooth, so dark and rich that she felt the compelling urge to reach out and touch it, to feel it under her fingers like she would a piece of fabric on display in a store. His black quick intelligent eyes were filled with humour and anticipation.

Her eyes lingered on the broad shoulders and long torso, and beyond that his thick dark inviting prick was impatient, throbbing, waiting for her to approach. His long, solid legs were stretched out along the full length of the bed. The rude scars on his hip were the flaw that anchored the rest of him in reality. He flushed, then squirmed under her unembarrassed exploration of him.

Not bothering to undress, she climbed onto the bed beside him. The audacity of her examination of him excited her and freed her from the role of passivity that she always adopted. She felt masterful and in control.

The surging power rising in her spirit went out to him like a challenge. The stickfighter accepted.

He pinned her under his bulk and kissed her, stroking her lips, forcing her to give him her tongue. The *gayelle* that sprang up around them roared. The *Maître* was on the offensive. He forced her bra down under the curve of her breasts, to her nipple—a blow! To the collarbones that pierced the skin of her neck—a blow! The *Maître* held his victim trapped against the bed, and the crowd went wild. Each assault of tongue and hand and *bois* left her giddy and drunk. The *flambeaux* with their greasy flames flickered on the insides of her eyelids, and their black smoke rose in her nostrils.

"No surrender," he said, and then she knew that he saw the *gayelle,* too. She hoped he would be merciful.

The arena became a bed again. She fought for breath in air that seemed to have become too thin for breathing.

"God," she whispered as though recognising divinity in the spark that arced between them. The sweat trickled out of her hair and ran down the sides of her face like tears.

Slim

Never mind the fucking rain. He splashed through the rising water in the yard without a care for the red mud that clung to his boots and speckled his jeans. Water coursed down from his jute hair and got into his eyes and his mouth. The stupid dog from the lady in the yard bolted gleefully out through the gate that he'd left open behind him.

"Fuck," he said as he watched it go. Too bad. Let it go dashing out, get itself killed down in the road. Or fall into the drains that had already started overflowing onto the pavement. So long as it didn't piss on his tires. Not that it mattered in this rain. His lips peeled back over his teeth in a grin.

This shit with Myra would be all over now. That's how you had to do it with them. Give them some time, let them cool down and start to miss the sugar. Then you turn up when they least expect it, and you got it made.

He banged forcefully on the door. The wind snatched her name from his lips and buffeted it away, so he tried again. "Myraaa!" He banged on the door again. He should just kick the fucking thing down and walk in, that's what he should do. Really surprise her.

He was sizing up the door for a kick when it suddenly opened. Myra's daughter was standing there, looking like hell, all skinny and shit with these black circles all round her eyes. What was Myra feeding the girl? He grinned at her. "Where's your mother?"

Chick gave him a look like he was shit or something. The rain pounded into the porch and onto his back. "You going to let me in?" Bitch just glared at him.

"Look, sister," he told her, real quiet because he wasn't here to start any trouble, not yet. "Look, where your mother is? Tell her I want to see her. Go and call her for me, okay?"

She curled her black eyes up at him. "Not here."

He put his hand up along the top of the door, just in case she decided to try to slam it in his face. "Look, just call her for me, okay?" He was going to stop being nice any minute now, and where would that leave her?

"If I tell you she's not here, then she's not here." She made a move to shut the door. Like he didn't see it coming. His hand on the door stilled her.

"Baby, she can't not be here. Not in this weather. You take me for a fool?" His slitted eyes warned her not to answer that.

"She . . . is . . . not . . . here." The girl held her hand up under his face like she wanted him to snap it off for her.

"Where then?"

"Don't know."

"Where?"

"You heard me."

He spun round, off the little porch and back into the rain, shouting Myra's name. She was here. He knew it. A stone under his foot caused him to stumble. He picked it up and threw it at the front window. The window shattered with a noise that made him feel warm in spite of the rain. He found another and threw it, found another and threw that.

The stupid girl was running out in the rain and shouting at him to stop. Waving her skinny arms in his face. He turned his attention to another window.

Then the door of the little house behind the building, the one small enough to be a shithouse, opened, and Myra was running out with this blouse on and no bra, with her hair all over the place. The shock alone had him laughing.

She ran out into the yard towards him, up to her ankles in mud. The cripple followed her in just his pants. Her mouth was open and she was shouting something that he couldn't hear. He was too busy looking at the daughter, at the look on her face at the sight of her mother coming out of this man's house with no underwear on. The girl's eyes could have popped out of her head.

When Myra came closer, he looked down at her belly and realised she hadn't done it yet. Her belly was round and high, and when he realised that after he'd gone through all that trouble to get the money for her, she still hadn't done it, he stopped laughing.

He raised a hand that was shaking with his rage and pointed it at the hump in her middle. "You didn't do it!" he told her. The wind tugged at his words. "I told you to do it! I told you!"

The girl next to him turned her burning eyes on his face. "Do what?" she was yelling. He ignored her and took a step closer to Myra. The cripple took a step towards *him*, fixing for a fight. That alone would have set him off laughing again, if things weren't so serious. "I told you to do it!" he told her again, and she was watching him with this stubborn look. Just like her daughter.

The girl kept looking from him to her mother's belly and back to him again. Her face looked like it was going to melt and slide clean off her head. "Do what?" she said again, although he could see that she knew very well do what. So he didn't answer.

"Get away," Myra was telling him with the same mouth she'd once used to lick the salt off his skin. "Out! Out!" Over and over, like she was singing in church.

"Do it!" he said again. The coward leatherman turned and ran back to his house, giving up on her. Slim was surprised at how fast he could move. Myra spun round in shock like she got a chair pulled out from under her, giddy. Stupid if she thought the old man would stand up to him for her.

But then he was back out of the house with this big stick in his hands, both hands, holding it up in front of his face with the rage of the devil in his eyes. Slim recognised the heavy black stick for what it was, and decided it was time to move. If he wanted her, he could have her. No harm done. Let him raise the bastard if he wanted that pussy so much.

When he turned to go, the daughter wasn't there anymore. Myra didn't look like she noticed she had gone. The man with the stick was standing in front of Myra with the stick up before his face, so Slim moved quickly, past the house where the boy was standing with his mouth open. The big white chicken was on the low wall, dripping wet, and as he passed it, he snatched it up, snapping its neck between his hands and tossing it at the boy's feet. Crunch, it went under his hands, like a dry twig. He grinned.

As he pulled away from the pavement, he looked back in the mirror to see the idiot boy cradling the twitching dead bird in his hands, and Myra, with the blouse wet and clinging to her body, looking round and round, turning her head this way and that, looking for her daughter.

Rory

When Gracie stilled in his arms, he laid her on the porch wall. Her muddied feathers curled with the damp, and her long feet were clenched. He stared at the dirty white bundle for a very long time and all the while his mind whirred frantically, trying to seek out and pin down the emotions which he knew were there but which eluded him. Shouldn't there be grief, horror, rage? Loss?

There was nothing, only some kind of fuzzed blur that reflected darkly, as in glass. He turned towards the yard where the bizarre scene had played out. Myra and the leatherman were still there in the rain. They had not moved. Myra stood with her blouse plastered to her skin and her hands up over her face. Jacob stood close to her with his staff in one hand, trying to wipe away tears that were replaced by the rain as quickly as he dried them. He couldn't see Odile.

He stepped out into the yard towards them, oblivious of Myra's state of undress. That they had emerged from the house in that condition did not strike him as unusual or remarkable. He came to stand close to the two. He had no sense that he was intruding.

"Where's Odile?" he asked.

Myra shook her head.

"In the house?" He had to shout over the wind, which by

now was working itself into a formidable rage. Myra didn't know.

The sound that roared around them seemed to have been torn from the throat of a huge animal. There was a splitting and a trembling of the air. *Fire,* he thought, *raging down the hill and headed right for us.* Before the flawed logic of this instinctive thought could hit him, the uppermost branches of the tamarind tree came down with a wrenching sound, splitting the trunk down the middle. The branches crashed noisily onto the centre of Myra's apartment. Glass, wood, brick, roofing splintered and flew into the air like an explosion. He felt debris flying past him, humming and whizzing; coarse splinters pierced his skin. He heard Myra's terrified screams, and turned towards the house thinking Odile, Odile, Odile.

The branch had shattered the front of the building and staved in most of the roof. He picked his way frantically through the broken furniture, slipping on the rug that was rapidly becoming sodden, avoiding fallen bricks and glass. Odile.

Myra and Jacob were close behind. Through the chaos they searched. Shrill, terrified screaming from the back of the house led them to Sebastian, who was cowering in his room with his hands over his ears. He was passive in Jacob's arms as he lifted him like a doll or a woman and picked his way back out again, into the rain and in the direction of his own house.

Rory looked for Odile. He and Myra ran from room to room, calling. The sodden tamarind branches stank. From room to room; she was not under the beds nor under the branches nor in the bathroom or the kitchen. Even when they realised the search was useless, her mother still called hoarsely. He looked at her and realised she was shivering from the damp and the cold and the terror.

"You stay," he told her. He put both hands on her shoulders in an effort to stop her from shaking. He felt tremors run through her body under the thin cloth. "Dress. Put something dry on. I'll get her."

"But where?" her mother wailed.

"I'll get her," he said. "I'll bring her back." And then he was out in the rain again.

The path to the river had become a river itself. The water rushed against his ankles, threatening to throw him down and sweep him away. It was madness for her to even try to go down there, but he knew she had.

He didn't bother calling; she wouldn't have heard. The thick brown water coursed down from up in the hills with its loot of garbage, leaves, and debris. He could hear the breath rasping painfully in his throat as he fought to maintain his balance, down through razor grass that slashed at him. He put his hands out before him blindly. Covered by swirling brown water, the way to their rock looked so different.

She was standing there on the highest point of the bank. Water rose to her calves. On the other side, their rock was barely visible above the gushing river.

He shouted her name again and again until he was right next to her. She glanced at him and turned away.

"Odile!" His hand closed about her upper arm.

She looked at him with eyes that sank all the way into her head.

"Come home," he said.

"Can't," she said.

"Come home."

"No."

"Odile." He put both hands on her shoulders and kissed her clumsily on the lips, hungry in spite of himself.

"She lied. He told her to do it and she didn't."

"Do what? What did he tell her to do?"

"She's pregnant."

"I know." He tried to kiss her cold mouth again.

"He told her to kill it."

"Who did?"

"Slim."

"And she didn't."

"No."

Rory rubbed his hands vigorously down her arms. She must

be dying with the cold. Even he was feeling the chill penetrate to his bones. The air in his head was expanding again.

"So what?" he asked.

"She wanted me to do it to mine. How could she want to keep hers and not want me to keep mine? She's selfish. That's what she is."

He was confused. "She what?"

"She wants me to kill it. But she won't kill hers."

"Your what?"

"My baby."

He heard the tamarind tree falling all over again. Crashing into him instead of the house. He reached out to take her in his arms. "Odile," he whispered. He pulled her to him. "I won't let her."

"What do you mean?" She was unmoving.

"She can't kill it. I won't let her."

"Why?" She was truly puzzled.

He whispered close to her ear, with reverence. "Because it's ours." The unbelievable magic of the words danced on his tongue.

Her laughter cut into him like barbed wire, shredding his mind. "You what?" she shrieked. He felt her breasts shake against his chest as she laughed. "You what?"

He was bewildered. He took a step back so that he could see her face.

"You what?" she was saying. "You think it's yours?" She was a madwoman. All reason was gone. "How could it be yours? Are you stupid?"

Fine cracks were forming in the glass.

"Are you stupid? We only did it last week! You think if it was yours I would know already? Don't you know *anything?*"

"It has to be mine," he managed faintly. Crack, crack, crack.

"Look, fool . . ." She tore herself from him and stood back. Her eyes were the eyes of someone who had gone a step beyond the frontiers of her soul. "I was pregnant long, long before I let you do it to me. Long before."

"It was our first time," he told her. He knew it to be true.

"*Your* first time," she corrected him.

His voice was faint. "You said you loved me."

"*You* said it." The crazy water swirled around them like blood.

The glass shattered. He heard the final explosion and felt the shards flying into his brain and lodging in his mouth and nose and ears. They pierced the backs of his eyes. The walls around his private universe collapsed under the pressure of the years. Finally, there were the feelings that had names but no sensation. There was the hurt. There was the rage. There was the loss. He was able to put the names to the faces for the first time and he was amazed at how sharp and bright and clear they were. They each had their own colour.

The first time he hit her, he hit her in the mouth, to stop her from laughing. The sound was cut off abruptly. The second and third times he saw the names of the feelings written in their colours across her astonished face. When she fell forward into the mud, he hauled her to her feet again. She wasn't crawling away, oh, no. He dragged her by the arm up the bank to a place where the water couldn't reach, and let her drop to the ground. She was crying. He kicked her and it felt good, so he kicked her again. Her belly was soft and yielding under his feet, like a big rotten fruit. He heard her voice going endlessly on and on, and she never stopped to take a breath, just screamed in one long continuous flowing note that went on until the blood started coming, coursing down her legs and down the bank to join their river. When he was tired, he stopped.

Jacob and Rory

Jacob stood by the window of his apartment and watched the boy. He was glad to be back in his small house, glad for the yellowed pages that surrounded him on all sides. He drew strength from them. Many passages, which he had come to know by heart, offered him comfort.

"I told her mother I'd bring her back," Rory said bleakly.

The boy sat on the floor with his back against the wall and his head in his hands. It was fully night, but neither of them wanted the lights on. The pelting rain had slowed to a drizzle. Jacob nodded, but Rory didn't see. "Yes," he said.

"I brought her back."

"Yes."

The boy's massive shoulders heaved. Under the still-damp shirt, Jacob saw his prize-fighter's muscles tense. "I didn't mean to do what I did. I didn't want to. It was the walls."

Jacob stilled the query on his tongue and stood silently, watching him. He let him finish.

"They came crashing down and I couldn't get out of the way. I couldn't stop them." The swollen face twisted again. Jacob listened to him choking on his grief, but didn't make a move.

He watched the boy's hulking form and remembered vividly that night in Sangre Grande when the smell of the burning *flambeaux* and the roar of the mob had gone to his head, when he'd lit into a young stickfighter and brought him to his knees, then flat on the ground. His bloodlust had exploded in his brain, and they'd had to tear him off the unconscious man as he beat him first with his stick and then with his bare fists. There had been no malice behind it, no quarrel, no grudge, just the blood on his fists that stank so strongly, he could taste it on his tongue.

He knew what Rory had felt out in the rain. It was a fighter's rage, fueled by a lifetime of insulation and denial. He watched Rory's huge hands as they hung limply at his sides, and cringed at the thought of what they had done to Odile's face. The vision angered him, but the complete instinctive understanding of Rory's pain and horror was just as acute. He wished he could say something, stand in the breach left by his uncaring father, and calm the boy's agony.

"Things are crashing down all over," he said, knowing that it wouldn't help.

The boy looked up in surprise. The idea that he wasn't the only one suffering seemed to be new to him. He looked down again.

From the window he could just see the top of the tamarind tree balanced on the ruined house. He wondered when Myra would be home. He didn't expect Odile to be released for some time.

Sebastian was over at Jillian's house; hopefully he would be asleep. The other two apartments had escaped with little damage, and were sound and dry enough to sleep in. As for Myra's—they'd have to see in the morning.

He watched the rear windows of Rory's place. The lights were out. He wondered if Rory's father was off drinking, or whether he'd just given up on the boy and gone to bed. Wasn't his problem; just his son's.

It horrified Jacob, this indifference. The man had not asked how Odile would be. He had offered no help when Rory had returned with the unconscious girl in his arms. Had shown no surprise, no anger, nothing. He'd simply turned an unidentifiable stare on Rory's shocked and exhausted face, and walked in through his door and pulled it shut. The boy had been living in an emotional vacuum. Jacob was certain he would have preferred a beating to this indifference.

"Think I'll go to jail?" the boy asked softly.

Jacob detached himself from the window and moved over to him. He put a hand on the back of his head. "They don't put boys in jail, son," he said.

"A home, then." Rory had not stopped trembling.

"I don't know."

Rory nodded and was quiet for a while. "Will the police come?"

"Nobody called them."

"Will the hospital call them, when they see what happened to her?"

"I don't know."

"Terrible, not to know," he said.

Jacob nodded. Again, the boy did not see him.

Rory left soon after, trudging heavily throughout the thin drizzle to his own house. He walked with dread in each step. Yet Jacob knew he had been anxious to leave, to ensure that he was out of the house before Myra came home. He wondered if he would ever be able to face her.

She came in after one in the morning. Jacob watched from the window as she alighted from the taxi and walked in through the open front gate. Jillian's dog had returned, and barked perfunctorily from the relative dryness of the porch. She walked right past her own home without so much as a sideways glance, picking her way around the shattered tree trunk and branches that lay across the yard. She made no attempt to cover her head or pull her light jacket closer around her.

He had the front door open for her by the time she reached the porch. He held out his arms and she fell into them gratefully.

"I need you," she said.

"I'm here," he said. He led her inside and pulled the door shut.

Odile and Myra

There were no sheets on the bed. The nurse said they simply
didn't have any. So Odile lay on the filthy mattress in her
cubicle and tried to screen out the sights and sounds of the
ward. The stench of urine, pigeon droppings, and decay ema-
nated from every wall. The feeble attempts by the hospital
authorities to improve conditions over the years had had little
impact on the depressing aura of disrepair, ineptitude, and
death.

There'd been no room in the maternity ward, and none in
the pediatric ward, either. As a result, she had found herself
relegated to the women's geriatric ward. All around her the
old and the dying groaned in their beds. Lonely old women
with no visitors lay listlessly on their dirty mattresses, wishing
someone would pass to touch their hands or comb their hair.
All around her, shriveled carcasses curled up on their beds,
waiting for death.

Odile wished that the curtain racks around her bed actually
bore curtains, so she could pull them around her and block
out the view of the other beds. She lay on her back looking
up at the stains on the ceiling. It shocked her that for the first
time in ages she'd been able to sleep.

When she looked down again, her mother was there. Myra
wore her sober brown dress and brown leather sandals. The

dress was becoming tight around her middle. Soon she would need to be buying fuller clothes.

For a moment Odile was surprised; her mother should have been in town selling her sandwiches. What would happen to the business? Her surprise was washed away by a flood of childlike relief. She felt like a little girl who'd fallen down and bumped her head. Mama to the rescue. Her bruised face throbbed.

Myra took her limp hand in her own strong ones and stood silently by the bed. Odile felt that her mother was waiting for her to speak.

"What about the house?" She'd remembered being brought back in Rory's arms, him sobbing noisily all the way, and being laid down on Jillian's front porch. The yard looked like God had put his hand down from the sky and just knocked everything over. That's why they didn't take her to her own house, she remembered. There was a tree in the house.

"We'll manage," Myra said. "Jacob will . . . help." She shifted nervously.

Odile could see Jacob in a clean white long-sleeved shirt and neat gray pants hovering at the entrance to the ward. He was twisting an old-fashioned gray fedora in his hands. He looked like he was dressed for church. He wasn't carrying his staff.

"He's good at that," she said to her mother. "Fixing things."

"Yes," Myra replied. "He's good."

Odile looked up at her mother through muddy water. How did things get so complicated? She wanted to cry.

"I'm staying with him," Myra said. "Until the house gets fixed."

She sensed that her mother was waiting for her permission. For her approval. She nodded, but did not say anything.

"What about Rory?"

"I haven't seen him."

"Is he in trouble?"

"I don't know."

Odile saw the two of them again, both distorted by their own misery, raging at each other on the riverbank. They'd become monsters that evening. They'd both attacked with the worst weapon at their disposal. She wondered how long his wounds would take to heal. She searched herself for anger and found only grief and sorrow.

"I think they're moving out. His father's leaving."

"Oh." She nodded. "I wonder if he'll come and see me."

Myra's hand tightened around Odile's. "You want to see him?"

"I don't know." She wondered if, after the mess that they'd made of everything, they would able to speak again. They'd never be friends, she knew that. Still, she worried about the idea of him wandering away unanchored, like a time bomb triggered by his own unhappiness. The thought bothered her.

"It mightn't be a good idea to see him," Myra said.

"Maybe not," Odile agreed. *Be well, my friend,* she thought. They were silent for a while.

"It's dead, you know," Odile said at last. "Satisfied?" There was an edge to her teeth. Instead of an uninvited presence, there was a vast emptiness in her belly. The emptiness left her feeling surprisingly hollow.

Myra winced. "No," she said. "I'm not satisfied."

"Well," she was petulant now, "I just thought it was what you wanted." She tried to ignore the burning behind her eyes. There was a sense of loss that she never would have expected. It puzzled her. Wasn't it what she herself had wanted? That it would all just go away?

Myra sat with difficulty on the edge of the thin foam mattress. The ancient metal bedsprings groaned and sank under her weight. "It's not what I wanted, and God knows I wouldn't have chosen it to be this way. I was just worried for you. You have a future. You're a bright girl. I didn't want you throwing away your life."

"Like you did with me?" This time there was no challenge in her voice, only a timid need for reassurance.

It was time to put and end to this issue, Myra thought.

When they'd last tried to bring it out into the open, none of the words had come out right. She spoke slowly, making sure she was understood. "That was different, Odile. Times were different. You have more chances now. And I don't regret what I did for you. You understand?"

Miraculously, the girl nodded.

Myra went on. "I'm happy with my life. I mean, I can be happy when things are okay again. With the house." She paused for a while. "And okay with you."

"They're not okay."

"I know. I want to know if they will be."

"I don't know." She wasn't ready for talking yet. It was going to take a lot of talking.

The nurse busied herself around Odile's bed, doing nothing much. She kept casting 'time-to-leave' looks in Myra's direction. Odile looked directly at her mother in panic. She didn't want to be alone again, not in this big gray sad place. She felt six years old. "You're coming again?" Her eyes were wide and anxious.

"Tomorrow," Myra assured her. She had to uncurl Odile's fingers from around her hand to release herself. "We'll talk some more tomorrow," she promised.

"Yes," Odile said. She watched as her mother walked slowly to the door where Jacob was waiting. Jacob placed the hat firmly upon his head, freeing his arms to embrace Myra. Silhouetted in the doorway, they faced each other. The bump of Myra's belly got in the way of the hug, but Jacob didn't seem to mind. They released each other with reluctance and proceeded with the other visitors towards the stairs. Odile watched until they were out of sight.

Jacob and Myra

He put his arm across her bowed shoulders. Her drawn face was distant and contemplative, and he wished he could go where she was in her mind, to offer help and support. Her brown eyes were like clouds.

"Her face will heal," he said. He desperately hoped he was right, and that the girl's beauty would not be marred.

Myra nodded. The hospital smelled of pigeons.

He wished she would take his hand. Eventually he made the move and took one of hers in his, a little embarrassed by this public demonstration. He couldn't bear to have what he felt for her laid out in public to be mocked by others. Old twisted man like him. But the busy crowds that thronged in the corridors took no notice.

They walked down the flights of stairs and out into the courtyard, away from the smell of pigeon shit and disinfectant. She stopped. In the sunshine her brown hair gleamed, and suddenly he realised that he didn't care what people thought. He loved this beautiful woman with the dense brown hair and worried eyes, loved for the first time without vanity or power or lust. He wanted desperately to make things right for her. He bent forward slowly and let his lips brush her brow. Her face quivered for a second and he heard a mewing, soft, like a kitten's.

I love you, he wanted to say, but he couldn't, not yet.

Maybe he would, in time, but for now he wanted simply to get used to the awesome force of the raw emotion. He laid his head close to hers. *I love you,* he said again with his mind, and hoped she would hear. He looked down at her again, and she was smiling.

"I'll make things good for you," he promised.

Myra nodded. "Yes."

"For you and Sebastian and Odile and the baby." It was like a holy oath.

She nodded again. He saw the sun being reflected in her eyes. "Yes," she said again. They turned to walk towards the wide arch that led to the exit. As he walked, he noticed that his leg didn't hurt so much.

july

Rory

Their new apartment was musty. Paint flaked from the walls like dandruff and the bed was one of those old ones with a mattress stuffed with coconut fibers. The many itinerant residents who had preceded him had worn the mattress cover down till the prickly fibers protruded through it and irritated his skin as he lay. The mattress sloped towards the middle; no matter where he lay, he always awoke in the morning almost jackknifed in the centre of an uncomfortable hollow.

Each night he climbed into bed with the knowledge that sleep would bring the police crashing through his dreams with their howling dogs straining at the leash. Each night he ran through the St. Ann's valley, down to the river, his and Odile's river, until he was cornered, and as he stood panting at the edge of the river which had grown too deep for him to cross, pleading for clemency, the police laughed and let the dogs loose.

Rory accepted this mental torture and physical discomfort as a kind of purgatory on earth. He had a lot to pay for, and it was best that he began now. His father had moved them within a matter of days to the busy town of Arima, far enough from Port of Spain to preclude many chance encounters with Odile and her family in the street. The man never once mentioned the night the tree came down, never alluded to the irrational act that had caused them to flee, apart from grumbling frequently that it was Rory's fault that he now had to commute so far to get to work.

School would be out for the long vacation in just a matter of weeks, so it didn't seem to matter if he just stopped going. Next term he would begin to worry about school again. He hoped that he would find another school, any school, one that was out of Port of Spain, to minimise the risk of rounding a corner and encountering a pair of dark eyes that just might hold enough condemnation to kill him.

One day he had met Jillian from next door. She had been coming out of a taxi round by the Arima Dial, the giant white-pedestalled clock around which the town sprang. She looked like she was going shopping. She spotted him instantly, with some unerring feminine radar. The two of them stood, tensed like small animals preparing to flee, watching each other for any hint of a threat.

Finally, with his courage and his heart in his hands, he crossed the road between them. She eyed him warily as he came, and as he approached, he felt the bitterness of bile rise to the back of his dry throat.

"Jillian," he began uncertainly, and then corrected himself. "Miss Jillian."

She stared at him, suspicious as a cat.

"You good?" he asked politely.

She nodded but did not speak. He wondered miserably whether he was going to spend the rest of his life branded a monster. Finally she opened her mouth. "Yes, I'm good. You?"

"Good," he said. The traffic roared around them. He felt exposed, criminal, standing here under the Dial in the most public place in the city with someone from his old life, someone who Knew What He Had Done. "And Miss Cole?" he went on.

"She's fine," Jillian said. She shifted her parcels from one hand to the next, restless.

Rory nodded. He stepped into the void. "And Odile?"

Jillian shifted her parcels again, while Rory waited, wondering how he managed to stand there when there was no ground beneath his feet. He heard the breath being drawn sharply through her nostrils. "She came out of hospital." Jillian said.

"Good," Rory said.

"I think she's going to be all right."

"Good."

Jillian hemmed and hawed for a few moments.

"Tell her I said Hello," Rory said. "Next time you see her."

Jillian heaved her heavy parcels high into her arms and turned to go. She gave no indication that she had heard his request. "I have to go," she told him.

Rory nodded.

"Busy," she explained.

He stood there on the nonexistent pavement, endless nothing going on and on beneath his feet, and watched her until she was out of sight.

Sebastian

His wife sat on the edge of the bed, admiring the new paint on the walls of his room. "It's nicer than the old colour," she assured him. "Much nicer."

"It goes with your dress," he said, and she blushed.

The house was all new. There were new windows and a new roof and it smelled of fresh paint. The lovely warm smell made him think of Christmas, and sometimes he liked to stand extra close to the walls with his face up against them and smell the new paint.

He sat close to her, humming to himself. "It isn't raining today," he said excitedly. "It didn't rain all day. I went down to the river, and guess what I found."

"What?" she asked, eyes shining like a young girl's.

"Look," he told her. He rose slowly and walked to the little basket that he used now instead of the pram that he couldn't seem to find. He came back with a small smooth stone in his hand. "Look." He held it out for her to see.

"Oh, it's *nice*," she cooed. He loved the softness of her voice.

"Take it," he offered, but she shook her head.

"No, you keep it. I can see it when I come to visit."

Sebastian nodded. He rose and walked over to the basket again, where he replaced the pretty stone. When he turned towards the bed, she was gone. He smiled. He knew she'd be back. He slung the basket over his arm and patted his neat brown hat onto his head. He shut the door behind him and walked past the living room, out the front door and into the street. He took up his position at the side of the road, looking expectantly in the direction that the kids would be coming. School would be out any minute.

ABOUT THE AUTHOR

Roslyn Carrington still has in her possession the book she wrote at age nine, a collection of stories, jokes, and games that she penciled on the pages of a small black notebook stolen from her grandmother's kitchen. The appreciation of her classmates encouraged her to try her hand at a dozen other novels over the next seven or eight years; most of these early pieces of writing have (perhaps mercifully) been lost to posterity.

She went on to earn a First Class Honours degree in Language and Literature from the University of the West Indies, receiving no less than seven academic awards, and earning the title of Student of the Year in both her second and final years. It was only after completing her tertiary education that she began seriously considering writing as a career.

She is a Trinidadian who has traveled extensively, but chooses to live and work on her native island. She leads what amounts to a double life; a mild-mannered public relations professional by day, she transforms into a pencil-gnawing, Thesaurus-throwing writer by night. Since 1996 she has penned a weekly opinion column in Trinidad and Tobago's most established newspaper, *The Guardian.* In addition to *A Thirst for Rain,* she has written a collection of short stories tentatively titled *Sex and Obeah.*

Roslyn Carrington shares her life with a wonderful man who steadfastly supports her in the pursuit of her dreams, and who shows remarkable understanding and patience on those nights when finding le mot juste seems to her to be the only thing that matters.

She looks eagerly forward to her future as an author, and anticipates a long and rewarding romance with the written word.

She can be reached at:

Roslyn Carrington
4405 N.W. 73rd Avenue
Suite #011-1241
Miami, FL 33166-6400

Or visit her Web site at www.roslyncarrington.com or E-mail her at roslyn@roslyncarrington.com.